BLUE FATE 3
DROPOUT

CASS TELL

BLUE FATE 3
DROPOUT

A novel from the Blue Fate series

destinēe media

PROLOGUE

Amsterdam, The Netherlands
July

Dick McDowell knew he found something big. In all his years of auditing, he had never seen anything like this.

He wiped his palms on the smooth desk top, leaving a slick line of sweat that quickly vanished in the heat. He closed his eyes for a minute to let the numbers register.

And then he grinned knowing he would not give this information to Unipac.

* * *

McDowell was on a special assignment. He was an independent auditor who did contract work for different auditing companies. In this case, it was for Stewart-Graves Financial Services out of London. He had been hired to do a rush job. Two large companies were on the brink of a merger. One was EuroVinco a European conglomerate. The other was Unipac, a diversified technology company from California. Unipac had engaged Stewart Graves to audit all of EuroVinco's operations. The last remaining piece was the EuroVinco Trading Company based in Amsterdam, and McDowell had been employed. He had worked for Stewart-Graves before.

After three days of working in the EuroVinco Trading department downstairs he had finished late last night—so late he had missed the happy hour specials at the local bars. And then this morning he had walked up the stairs into the second floor office.

Half a dozen men sat behind nondescript desks in the front room. A short, dark man with a big nose scowled and put down his falafel sandwich. "This office only for employees. Who are you?"

"My name is Dick McDowell, of Stewart-Graves Financial Services. And I'm here to audit you. Congratulations." He made a mock bow with his briefcase still in hand and started past the wall of filing cabinets for one of the three empty offices lining the back wall. Each office sported a large window for keeping tabs on the bland beige room where the men were now exchanging glances.

The one whose sandwich lunch had been interrupted shoved back his chair and stopped McDowell at the far right office door. "My name is Ziginiglou, Mr. Gingiz Ziginiglou. Here is separate department—separate company from downstairs. We share building, but that is all." He attempted a civilized smile.

"What's the name of this company then?" McDowell asked.

Ziginiglou paused, "EuroVinco Trading, but…"

"For your information," McDowell said slowly, enunciating as if speaking to a child, "I was told to audit EuroVinco Trading, Amsterdam — subsidiary of the big and famous EuroVinco Corporation, and you," he jabbed a finger at Ziginiglou, "are part of EuroVinco Trading—a little bitty piece in that corporate pie, but still a piece. So you"—another jab—"will be included in the audit." He smelled garlic on Ziginiglou's breath.

A thick vein budged along Ziginiglou's forehead. "You don't understand. This is Specialized Trading Department. We have same name with downstairs, but we are, we are…" he waved his arms, "we are separate legal entity. Maybe you instructed to audit them, but we no receive instructions for audit."

Dick McDowell narrowed his eyes and looked down his nose at Ziginiglou. Both men were overweight, but McDowell was twice as large and taller. "You are the one who doesn't understand. I was assigned by Stewart-Graves who is helping your big bosses in the EuroVinco Corporation to marry the famous Unipac of Silicon Valley. What do you think they are going to do when I tell them that an uninformed little runt is trying to stop me from doing my job? I am going to look through any and every piece of paper in this department, and then I am gonna make a nice big report. If you get in my way, I will get on the phone to Stewart-Graves. They will call your big bosses and tell them some uncooperative onion-eater over in Specialized Trading is obstructing the wedding plans. Don't know about you, but I wouldn't count on any promotions after that."

A balding, grim-faced man, who had been absorbed in his computer screen, stood up and motioned to Ziginiglou who went over to the man's desk. After whispering with him for half a minute, Ziginiglou walked back to McDowell without looking at him.

"Please wait while I make telephone call."

★ ★ ★

He was given the go-ahead and he set up shop in one of the empty offices. And then he raided the filing cabinets, and finally was armed with records of EuroVinco's orders and payments to suppliers and customers. From McDowell's windowed office he could watch the back of Ziginiglou's head. At 9:00 a.m. his office had been completely empty except for a desk, chair, phone and wastebasket. By 5:00 p.m. it was beginning to look and smell just the way he liked it.

He picked at one of the two overflowing ashtrays, looking for a smoldering butt to puff. One found, he reached for a half empty cup of stone-cold coffee. Then leaning back in his chair, he heaved his feet up onto a damp, browned stack of notebooks. Earlier he had knocked coffee across his desk. Five crumpled paper cups lay in and out of paperwork, and three more lay in the corner close to the trashcan. He was a lousy shot, had never been good at basketball. But he was dead on with the numbers and that's all that mattered.

And these numbers were something. Heads were going to roll. Unlike the downstairs department, this one was a maze. Downstairs they distributed electronics parts and collected payments. All of their money went straight to the local EuroVinco bank accounts. Upstairs they distributed steel pipes to Iraq, insecticide to Columbia, chemical processing equipment to Sudan and North Korea, and coffee to Somalia—and a few more things to a few more countries, which shouldn't legally be receiving Western imports.

Payments from these companies were made to a EuroVinco accounts at three different banks: Deutsche Bank, Credit Agricole, and HSBC. Then suspiciously hefty sums were transferred from those accounts to a numbered bank account at a discrete private bank called Conquest Bank. McDowell wondered why those transfers were made and who was the account holder at Conquest Bank?

On several invoices from suppliers he came across the name ET Sports Investment. Their pale blue invoices looked legit. The company logo was formed by two golf clubs, crossed to form an 'X,' at the center of which a soccer ball, basketball and baseball converged in the shape of a three-leaf clover. The EuroVinco Specialized Trading department received five digit billings from ET Sports Investment for such things as "advisory services" and "10,000 units" and "Eight metric tons". Indeed these were strange items from a sports company. They paid out what seemed to be clean EuroVinco Corporation money for these charges to an account in London—a Conquest Bank account.

ET Sports Investment was not the only company to acquire large sums of money from Specialized Trading for unspecified or strange merchandise. One company took payments for goods simply listed on every invoice as "specialty products" and another was reimbursed "in U.S. dollars only" for "sand and water." The payments again went to accounts at Conquest Bank.

This was highly unusual that huge payments would be going to various accounts at one small discrete private bank. That set off red flags in the auditor's mind. And it was definitely suspicious that business was being conducted with black-listed countries, for goods that didn't make sense. This was the kind of information that Unipac would be highly interested to know about. It was also the kind of information that the account holders at Conquest Bank would be willing to pay to hush up. McDowell was more interested in the second option.

Ziginiglou had handed over these stacks of papers with a tight-lipped grimace. He'd been as uncooperative as mild discourtesy allowed. And he had likely not even handed over the stuff that would complete this puzzle.

Dick crumpled his coffee cup and grabbed for a pen. On a blank piece of paper, he wrote something in large letters and taped it to the window facing the main office so that all the employees would see it when they came in the following morning. He cracked a laugh, then looked at his watch and noticed it was six o'clock in the evening. He decided to call it quits for the day. He hated working past six o'clock.

He marked several binders at incriminating pages, put the various invoices back into their respective folders and placed them in his briefcase. He took the elevator down and stepped out at the first floor office, breathing hard from the load of his overstuffed case. He used the back of his free hand to wipe away sweat that dripped from his temple. He needed a beer.

The receptionist was bent over her desk. McDowell tilted his head and took in her slim, blond, Dutch build. She was shutting her message pad and had her purse already slung over one shoulder. He could just see the top of her right breast where her shirt opened a bit as she moved.

"Hi, honey," McDowell said, still out of breath. "How about buzzing me up a taxi?" He coughed, bringing up phlegm and swallowing it again.

"Of course, sir." Her voice was polite and he thought the accent was sexy. She dialed the number and spoke a few brief sentences in Dutch. Hanging up the telephone she said, "The taxi should be here in about three minutes."

"That's quick," he raised one eyebrow, eyeing her down the slope of his nose. He thought she had that friendly look. Without time to spare, he gave her a gigantic yellow smile, which pushed his fleshy cheeks up so that his eyes almost disappeared.

"You sure get hungry after a hard day's work, don't you?" He asked.

It was hard to say whether he was winking or whether his eye was twitching. She answered, "Yes," narrowing her own eyes the slightest bit.

"How about dinner?" McDowell had leaned forward and rested his palms on her desk.

Readjusting her purse, she lifted her chin and declined, "Thank you sir, but I already have an engagement with my boyfriend." By the time she finished her sentence, she had come around her desk and was heading for the door.

"What's the matter honey, you don't like a good thing when you see it?"

The young woman paused with her hand on the door lever, "Have a nice evening, sir. The taxi should be here any minute."

When it came, McDowell, still mumbling about what the receptionist had missed, left the building and yanked open the cab door. Still hampered by the heavy case, he grunted and heaved himself into the back seat, barking, "Apollo Hotel."

★ ★ ★

A shower, a taxi ride to the Red Light District, and four beers later, McDowell was ready for some window shopping.

It was a late summer evening. Businessmen, tourists and college kids—both male and female—moved in and out of the neon-lit strip joints and sex shops that occupied the quaint old-world houses. Dick floated through the mass of bodies, admiring women in the various windows.

Finally frustrated by having his elbows jostled and his view blocked, he followed a couple into a French-style bistro. It was cozy with candlelight and the voice of Edith Piaf playing in the background. Groups of three or four sat around tables eating appetizers and laughing softly.

Three men entered the bistro not long after him—all of Amsterdam seemed to be out of the house tonight. The waiter seated McDowell and took his order for two beers and a Monte Cristo sandwich. When the sandwich came, he slathered it in jam and cut it into precise squares before devouring them. One of the three men cast a look of faint disgust in McDowell's direction.

At the next bar, decorated in British brick Tudor style, he had three martinis and a plate full of deep fried sardines. He munched the crunchy fish, trying to decide between a redhead he'd seen with a coiled tiger tattooed to pounce on her breast or a black-eyed beauty dressed as an elf, complete with pointed ears. Savoring the choice and his last sardine, he paid the bill and made his way back out into the swarms of people.

After a few blocks, he decided he needed to sit with a beer again, somewhere away from the noise. He made his way toward the quieter end of the street and turned into a dim alley just beyond the boundaries of the "district." This area was laced with canals whose evaporating water dampened and cooled the air. Several tourists passed in ones and twos and disappeared in the direction of the brothels. Out of the glare of red lights and neon, McDowell noticed that the night had grown quite dark.

He turned again onto a crooked street running alongside a canal. The façade of a bar he'd never tried, just across the water, caught his eye. He headed for the small pedestrian bridge that spanned the water in a considerable arc. He climbed the slope of it, using the railing to help him move his body upward.

A few lights flickered on either side of the canal. He watched the play of their reflections on the murky surface of the water, suddenly tired. Lights blurred and merged and returned to focus. He gripped the railing and realized how drunk he was.

As he regained his balance, he heard a shuffling sound from the far end of the bridge. A tramp had mounted it and was headed his way. The bridge was narrow; barely wide enough for two people of average build to pass at the same time. McDowell yelled, "Wait till I cross." The tramp continued slowly toward him. McDowell kept forgetting they spoke Dutch here.

McDowell reached the center of the bridge first and stopped. The tramp would not be able to fit past him, and there was no way that Dick McDowell was going to turn around. The tramp would have to go back, even if McDowell had to force him back with his own two hands.

He was sweating now, and fumbled in his jacket pocket for a

handkerchief. When he looked up, the tramp was just in front of him, staring at him. Despite the darkness, McDowell could see a raised scar curving from the corner of the man's left eye, across his cheek, toward his chin. His forehead was craggy with deep wrinkles. He moved in close to McDowell and stammered, "Would, would you have a few Euros to loan me for a meal?"

"Get a job!" McDowell snapped. "I don't give handouts to beggars." He attempted to shove his way past the tramp, but the man stood firm. McDowell stepped back, surprised.

A small smile crossed the tramp's lips. He held out a cupped hand and said again, "Just a few Euros?"

McDowell heard a noise behind him and was relieved to see that two men had begun to cross the bridge and were headed in his direction. He called out to them, "Hey! This crazy tramp's blocking my path. We can't all cross at the same time. We won't fit. Maybe you guys can get him to move out of the way."

The men quickened their pace and McDowell grinned back at the tramp. One of the men had a thick black moustache with a cigarette sticking out from under it and bore an odd resemblance to Joseph Stalin. The other one's skinny body was wrapped in a long coat and his eyes darted from face to face.

They looked beyond McDowell to the tramp who swiftly reached beneath his coat and pulled out a solid metal bar. Holding it in both hands, he struck a powerful blow to the back of the McDowell's head.

Things went black and he fell forward onto the bridge. His head bounced on the planks. The two strangers heaved him onto his side. He lay unconscious, his breath coming out in strangled wheezes.

The tramp searched McDowell's pockets and pulled out his wallet. He tossed various credit cards into the water and then held up a hotel key-card in a small envelope with "423" written across it. He smiled.

"Hurry Yass, take the money," the shifty-eyed one said to him, grabbing at the wallet before Yass threw it in the water.

Yass held the wallet up in the air and said, "Take it, Valentine."

Valentine lunged for it and missed. Yass put the wallet into his coat pocket.

Turk, the large Joseph Stalin looking man with the mustache, laughed under his cigarette.

The three of them struggled to lift up the heavy body. They managed to maneuver its sagging belly over the rail, which served as leverage when they lifted up the feet. With a strong push they slid the fat man into the water. The splash sent a series of waves lapping up against the sides of the canal.

They watched the water until it was still, only a few bubbles disturbing the surface, then left the bridge together and slid into a shadowy recess between two buildings. Yass looked up and down the street for witnesses, but the street had been empty. They reemerged and strolled along the edge of the canal to make sure there was nothing stirring in it. Then they separated and crossed the canal.

After several minutes Yass let out a low whistle and the other two joined him at an abandoned shop-front.

Valentine's eyelids twitched as he scanned the buildings' façades. "Damn you," he said to Turk. "If you had done your share of the lifting, I wouldn't have blood all over my shirt."

"I couldn't do any more than I did. You saw how big he was."

Valentine turned to Yass and said, "We could have used an extra hand."

Yass threw the fat man's wallet at Valentine. "Take his money and buy yourself a new shirt. We're wasting time, and I still need to make a telephone call. We meet later at the Apollo Hotel as planned."

They dispersed, blending casually into the darkness of the Amsterdam alleyways.

★ ★ ★

Shortly after the evening maid completed her rounds on the Apollo Hotel's fourth floor, a man entered room four twenty-three. His olive face bore a scar from the corner of the eye down to the chin. He slid a keycard through the reader and pushed the door open. After glancing into the bathroom and closets, he looked under the bed and behind the long curtains over the window.

When he felt sure the room was vacant, he opened Dick McDowell's briefcase and removed a number of papers and notebooks. He closed the briefcase and rifled through clothing and toiletries, leaving everything exactly as he had found it.

On his way out, Yass noticed a card lying on the pillow next to a wrapped chocolate. It read, "Pleasant Dreams, Compliments of the Apollo Hotel."

Yass took the chocolate and slipped it into the pocket of his jacket. The occupant of the room would not need it this night.

CHAPTER 1

Llanca, Spain
July

The train hissed to a stop alongside the open-air platform. A small man in gray trousers shuffled out of the white stucco station house, shouting *"Llanca, aqui."* Train doors slid open, and vacationers descended into the warm summer evening.

Justin Collins stood under the shade of a nearby umbrella pine, hands in his back pockets. He rose up on his toes, and a tree branch brushed his eyebrow. He was glad of his height as he easily looked over the old men in berets, round Germans and tall Dutch for Gloria's auburn hear.

He had dreamt of her last night. He had watched the red digits of his alarm turn 4:00 am. Then the numbers had merged into long strands of her hair, and she was reaching for him, gesturing for him to enter a door he recognized.

★ ★ ★

He thought of her now whenever he thought of trains. They had met on one last March. It was at a point when he was beginning to forget about his experience at Vine Industries. Sometimes the pain from that was very raw.

Justin had taken the regional commuter from Barcelona to Llanca. It was a Friday evening and half of the city—commuters and weekenders alike—appeared to be packed inside, headed for the beaches along the Costa Brava.

With no seats available, Justin stood in an entry compartment. He found himself wedged into a corner near an inflated turtle tube and the pigtailed two-year-old whose mother was attempting to keep her from "swimming" in it. The girl was the same age as his daughter Sophie.

He swallowed and looked into the car where seated passengers were barely visible through the standing ones. A squat man in plaid stood holding the back of a headrest. Justin looked at the seat's occupant and stared.

A young woman had fallen asleep. Her head lay to the side, thick reddish brown hair curling down her shoulders, reaching along the slope of her neck and the deep 'V' collar of her white dress. Justin found himself thinking of angels.

Her arms had slackened with sleep and he noticed that she was holding something. Just under her hand and ready to slip to the floor hung a document from a Spanish bank. He translated the words to be something like 'investment procedures.' A handbook of sorts, then. He had trouble picturing her as a banker. He preferred angel.

At the next stop, an old man in a wide-brimmed straw hat and carrying a grimy canvas bag entered the train. When the ticket controller came, the man had no ticket. As the conductor processed one for him, the man dug around in his bag for the fee. He was one Euro short.

Justin leaned over, a coin in hand, but the conductor shook his head and said, "Every day it's the same thing. These bums try to ride the train for free. You are just wasting your money." Justin insisted and paid anyway, feeling a faint blush begin across his cheeks. He noticed that most of the people in the car were watching him, including the young woman.

She had awakened, and Justin blinked when he saw the color of his own eyes mirrored in hers—jade green.

* * *

"Justin." Those two green eyes were in front of him now, lit with laughter. Justin realized the train was already pulling away.

"Hey. There you are," he smiled.

"I've been walking toward you, waving. Your mind must have been somewhere else?" She smiled up at him.

"Actually it was with you." He gave her a quick kiss, took the overnight bag from her shoulder and slipped it over his own. "How was the ride?" They drifted away from the platform and began to walk along the road toward town, following the general course of people who had disembarked from the train.

"Oh, crowded as usual. I read over the business pages so I could advise some of my clients about their stocks. I'm a little tired, but more than anything I'm hungry."

"Great. I was hoping you'd say that. A table should be ready for us at La Casa Brasa in about," Justin looked at his watch, "thirty minutes."

"You are good to me, Justin." She squeezed his arm. "Maybe we can stroll on the dock before we eat."

His forearm tingled at her touch and he laughed. "Sounds perfect. You are what they call in America 'low-maintenance.'"

"And what does that mean?" She stopped and faced him over her shoulder, hands on her hips. A silver hoop earring swung to a stop on the raised collar of her white cotton blouse.

"It means I want to spend time with you." As he said it, he felt his chest constricting. He had said the same thing to his wife Chantal.

⋆ ⋆ ⋆

La Casa Brasa balanced on a stony ledge between a sprawling villa and a tiny park, half way up the hill from the bay. Gloria had introduced Justin to it. He liked its stucco arches and the homey, no-frills ambience. Tonight they sat at their favorite table, in the corner by the window. They watched the sky over the Western mountains smolder orange, pink and violet as the sun set, streaking the rippled clouds that stretched into the sea.

"When I see this, I wonder why I still want to be in Barcelona," Gloria said, her voice almost reverent. She sipped her wine and selected a clam from her bowl of steamed shellfish, carefully removing its shiny center with her fork.

"I'm always in awe here too," he replied. "But not just because of the landscape." He poked the shell of a mussel with a knife, "I almost didn't stop in Llanca that first time."

He was silent a second, then began scraping at the shell's black brine. "Did I tell you I followed you off the train?"

"Today?" She finished chewing the clam. "But...."

"After I first saw you. When you got off here in Llanca. I followed you into the village. When you reached your home and went in, I felt like I had lost sight of land."

She looked out the window, pulling her slender fingers up and down the stem of her wine glass. He lifted his own hand to reach for hers, but an image flashed through his mind that made him stop. Chantal's hands—long, white and lean—flitting from her shoulder to her chin and out into the air in front of her, flying as fast as her French words, emphasizing each of them with a mysterious, playful sign language. The image disappeared as suddenly as it came but had completely distracted him. He stared at the wedge of lemon he'd squeezed of its juice. Gloria had said something. She tilted her head forward, no longer for an answer but to wait for him to return to the present.

"Sorry. I was just," he paused, "following a thought. I didn't hear what you said."

"It's fine. It means you have a strong imagination. I said I hadn't wanted to come here because I thought it was a little nowhere place— which shows you how narrow- minded we city people can be," she said.

Almost as an afterthought she added, "I did see you that night. From my window."

They ate in silence for several minutes. When the waiter took their order for crème caramel and coffee, Justin attempted to restart the conversation. "The days are so much longer than when I first arrived here, and the sunset seems to last forever." Scenery. He clenched his jaw. Almost as stupid as commenting on the weather.

"Yes, this is a beautiful time of the year," she replied, "but September is even more so."

"Why September?" He asked, grateful for her effort.

"By then the sun has started its journey to the south, yet the land is still dry from the summer heat. Then you can see those hills in the distance clearly." She made a gentle line in the air with her finger, drawing his attention to the horizon. "And, though you may not believe me, the colors of the sunset are more brilliant in the early fall."

"Yes, hard to believe." The colors reminded him of a painting Chantal had completed over a year ago when they went to Greece on holiday. He looked down and began to stir his coffee, though he had added nothing to it.

Gloria rescued him again. "And I suppose I like September because we have more time for ourselves to appreciate the beauty of this creation."

He glanced up. "How do you mean?"

Her eyes caught him off guard. They burned with an energy that seemed too vast for one person to contain. She tilted her head, her thick hair falling in loose waves over her shoulders, light reflecting off the reddish tones. He suddenly saw the Spanish hills flashing behind her as they had on the train. When he hadn't even known her name.

But now he knew her, had more than permission to touch her. He found himself reaching for a stray curl and pushing it back behind her ear. She smelled of Givenchy and shampoo.

She blushed. "I, um mean that in July and August visitors flood the village. By September, the crowds leave, and the locals who work the tourist industry can slow down. And now I am one of those locals. We chat longer in the street. We have more time in the morning to stop for a coffee before working. So I am still here, and it is a somewhere place after all."

"If I hadn't seen Llanca for myself, I would have thought you were a hopeless romantic." He sighed. Somehow touching her hair had stabilized him, brought him down on the far side of his uncertainty. Without thinking, he leaned across the table and kissed those red lips.

He knew what he would do.

CHAPTER 2

Paris, France
June, the previous year

He had no idea what to do. He'd woken up to find all of his undershirts in his sock drawer and all his ties in his underwear drawer. And she'd hidden the underwear.

"Chantal!" He yelled, heading for the parlor only to find her leaning in the bedroom doorframe. One arm rested up along the jamb, and the sleeve of her silk robe had fallen back to her elbow. The morning sunlight passed through the Parisian buildings and window behind her, as if only intent on lighting her pale hair.

"If I do not do this, you will become bored and leave me," she said, grinning.

"If you did not do this, I would be more likely to get to work on time," he said, but he couldn't help smiling. "I hope you are not teaching our daughter your tricks—so she can drive some poor man to distraction when she gets older."

"But of course I am! I said to her, 'Sophie, where shall I put papa's underclothes,' and she crawled toward the hall closet. So, I took her advice." As Justin went down the hall to the closet he could hear Chantal continue, "and she was very happy with the choice because she didn't cry all day."

When he opened the closet, he found his underwear neatly stacked in the laundry basket and on top of them a foil-wrapped chocolate heart, a handkerchief and a card. In the card, Chantal had written, 'So that you will remember my heart is with you today—a heart. So that your heart will be with me—my perfume. So they will not dismiss you from work—underwear.'

He sniffed the scent of Chanel on her handkerchief and folded it into his shirt pocket. Then he went back into the bedroom where she had stretched out on the bed and jumped next to her, sending her bouncing. She giggled as he covered her with kisses. Breathing heavily, he asked, "What makes you think you can keep winning my love like this?"

She stretched and brought her arms around his neck. He was so close he could see new freckles in the constellation across her cheeks that he knew by heart.

She lifted herself up and brought her lips close to his ear. She whispered, "Cheri, a thing won must be continually won forever."

He pulled down her robe and pulled up the bedspread.

★ ★ ★

He had a full day at Vine Industries. Flow-charts, secretaries, memos and contingency plans kept flying at his desk. He didn't even realize that he had skipped dinner until the phone rang. He answered, "Justin Collins speaking."

"Mon cheri, it's seven-thirty. Where are you? Sophie is waiting for a good night kiss. And so is her mama." He could hear her smiling.

"Oh darling. I'm sorry. I lost track of time. But it looks like I have a few more things to do. Is it OK if I make a late night of it here?" he asked, his eyes on a list of potential sites for the construction of a new plant.

"Ah, but you must come home and eat your dinner, so that you do not get too thin." She sounded worried.

He felt torn between going home and getting one last decision made, so he stalled. "Darling, I'm far from thin. I've put on quite a few pounds from sitting around conference tables every day."

"You see! Another good reason to come home," she said. "But wait one moment." He heard some whispers and then another voice came over the phone. It was Pete Vine.

"Justin, as your boss, I request you to come home and put out this fire in your kitchen." There was a short burst of laughter, and the phone went dead.

He was puzzled. Fire. What fire? Why was Pete Vine at his home?

Had he forgotten a dinner engagement? He flipped through his planner but found no record of a dinner with Pete.

When he reached home and walked through the front door, he saw a collection of his friends drinking wine in his living room—Pete and Dora Vine, Stefan Von Portzer, Charles Graves, Jean Marilleau, and Pierre Solet. As usual, Stefan was dressed in full evening kit, complete with cufflinks and an elegant, jeweled woman on his arm. She was holding Sophie and jiggling a doll at her. Justin stared at them for a moment and then said, "Uh, Hello."

"Chantal, your husband is home, and you really must see his face," Charles called in his clipped British accent.

"I'm coming," she answered from the kitchen. "Are you ready?"

"We're ready," the group responded in a scattered unison.

"What fire?" Justin asked, trying not to show how bewildered he felt.

Chantal pushed the kitchen door open, and, after a short delay, appeared holding a three-layer cake ablaze with thirty-two candles.

"Oh," Justin said. "My birthday."

"Yes, sweetheart, it is." Chantal beamed at him, kissing his earlobe.

Pete let out a deep laugh from his rounded middle, reaching up to squeeze Justin's shoulder. Stefan, standing next to him with the perfect posture of a supporting column, shifted his strong jaw line into mock rebuke. "Mr. Vine, you should not laugh. I believe the gentleman is suffering from long hours in your service." Pete waved an arm playfully at Stefan as if to shoo him away. Both men's eyes sparkled.

"I've worked with you for many years," Charles said to Justin, "and I know you to be a man who lives by his calendar. Now you are reaching the age where the little squares on the calendar confuse you."

"Quick! Quick! Let's all sing before the cake melts away!" Dora cheered. The entire group broke out in a dissonant but enthusiastic chorus of "Happy Birthday."

* * *

Later that week, Chantal called him from her studio. He recognized her number on the caller-ID pad and picked up the phone.

"Justin, I have the tickets. Be ready before eight."

As soon as he heard her voice, he was imagining her in the blue silk organza dress he'd bought her yesterday. Though he knew that even in the painting smock she was surely wearing, she would look fabulous.

It occurred to him she wanted a chance to wear her gift. Wait, eight o'clock tonight? "What tickets?" he asked.

"For a jazz concert. I hope you will like it."

"I have work, Chantal. I can't." But he put down his pen. He had just designed a business plan for the promotion of sales in Eastern Europe and was scribbling final adjustments. It was certainly more pleasant to picture his wife dressed for an evening out, hair up in a twist, neck free for her grandmother's broach. He loved to fasten it while she held back stray strands of hair.

"The saxophonist is quite famous," she assured him.

"Yes, but I have a presentation tomorrow morning at seven-thirty."

"Seven-thirty? On Saturday? Oh la la! And they say that we artists suffer."

"Our international marketing manager from California is flying through tomorrow. It's the only time we can have this meeting with the entire management team."

"You can still go to the meeting. You will be nice and relaxed after a grand evening out."

Her logic amused him. He could feel himself relenting though he tried one more excuse. "But I'm not familiar with French music."

"The musicians are from America." She laughed. "And you must wear your tuxedo."

CHAPTER 3

The concert that night turned out to be a fund-raiser for Unicef's child education programs. The Salon d'Opéra of Le Grand Hôtel Intercontinental was filled with men in their black-tie best and women arrayed in waterfalls of diamonds. Each couple had paid one thousand euros to eat a gala dinner donated by the hotel and drink fine wine, courtesy of politician-vintner Jacques Gaubert. The much-touted New Orleans band, Jam-buc-Blues, filled the Salon with rhythm for the Parisians and politicians who came to rub shoulders and be seen.

Justin turned from a platter of champagne flutes with one in hand. He cringed as he looked out over the room and took a drink, swallowing more than he'd intended. He was used to satisfying his social urges through power lunches and strategy dinners. He never felt well practiced in mixing with the European jet set.

Tonight especially, he felt too detached and preoccupied to enjoy the evening. He had not spent enough time preparing for the meeting tomorrow. He had the niggling feeling he had forgotten to consider some important trade law factors that would only come to him once the meeting was over.

He glanced at Chantal, whom he'd left chatting with a friend from the Paris art scene. She looked relaxed and radiant, her hazel eyes widening to emphasize a point. He forgot his anxiety for a moment as he admired the blue silk of the dress he'd chosen for her. It clung to her slender chest and hips just the way he had imagined in the office earlier. She must have felt his eyes on her, for she turned and blew him a kiss.

He walked over and, pushing her glossy blond hair aside, whispered in her ear, "How did you persuade me to come tonight?"

"Oh," she said, in an exaggerated mysterious tone, "It's well known that I have magical powers." She waved her hand in the air as if it held a wand capable of casting a spell. Sometimes he wondered.

"I can't seem to relax. Can't concentrate on the small talk," he continued, sticking a finger into his starched collar and draining his glass.

"*Ah, mon cher!* That is not stress! It's love." She winked. "You must relax."

As if on cue, they turned to find that Stefan Von Portzer had materialized in front of them. Chantal moved toward him, saying, "Ah, the art-collector who moonlights as a businessman. *Bon soir,* Stefan." They exchanged three kisses on alternating cheeks after the Swiss fashion.

Justin shook Stefan's hand when Chantal stepped back, relieved to see someone he knew. Stefan's black hair, peppered with gray at the temples, lay flawlessly across his well-shaped head. In his tux—or even in plaid—the man could have doubled for Sir Lawrence Olivier. Still, Justin had the impression that Von Portzer was lacking something tonight.

Stefan gestured at Justin with his glass. "We see each other twice in a week. It seems that you have started to become social after all." He smiled.

Justin laughed. "Against my own will. If left to my own devices, I'd have been in the office preparing a presentation right now."

"We should not speak of business on an evening like this." Stefan nodded at the whirring room of people slowly finding their tables.

"But how is the management of the Paris office going?" He faced Justin, but his eyes strayed over the crowd.

"Right now, I'm working on reaching the Eastern European markets," Justin said, following Von Portzer's gaze. It came to rest on the most striking woman in the room. Extremely tall, her olive skin was in full view where her wine-colored evening gown plunged low in front and back. She was posing amidst a group of men who looked to be on the verge of dropping their glasses—wine or eye glasses. Or both. She was stunning.

That's what Von Portzer was missing.

"Eastern Europe, you say?" Von Portzer seemed pleased. "You know, of course, that if you ever need mediation or advisory services, I may be able to assist you in that regard."

"Ah, Stefan. You are skilled at assisting anyone in any regard," Chantal said. "And well acquainted with the best of everything, in art and in life." She raised an eyebrow and then looked at the tall woman.

Von Portzer smiled slightly. "You have not met my friend from Morocco? Her name is Zoë. Together we are meeting a small coterie of dignitaries here in Europe. I must ask to be excused." He handed Justin a small white card. "I have a new number. Enjoy the concert— and yourselves." He nodded in farewell and turned to meet his "friend from Morocco."

Justin examined the business card, flipping it over. "Just a telephone number." He shook his head as they watched the retreating back of their friend. "It's true the Swiss treasure their privacy."

Remembering something, Chantal pulled at his arm, "He helped me to sell the new painting." Her eyes were wide with pleasure. They had hints of sapphire in them from her dress.

"The mother and child?" Justin asked, slightly disappointed. That had been a favorite from the moment he'd seen it. "Who's the lucky owner?" he asked, glad that she was pleased. It meant so much to her when someone wanted her work.

"Vine Industries, Paris office." She beamed, releasing his arm and standing back to get the full benefit of his reaction.

Justin didn't know what to say.

A waiter approached, carrying a tray of glasses bubbling with champagne. Chantal took two, handing one to Justin.

He finally spoke. "Congratulations. And thank you for keeping it close to home." He toasted her, sipped the pale liquid, and started to feel less tense.

He traced the chain of her broach to where it lay just above the hollow between her breasts. "By the way, how did you come across our tickets?"

"I traded a painting to Stefan for them." Chantal took a sip from her glass. With a swirl of her skirt, she caught his free hand and led him grandly to their table.

The musicians took the stage, blowing out long low riffs on saxophone and clarinet while waiters in white jackets and spats served the first course—*escargot*. Even after five years in Paris, the sight of the little snails lying curled in their shells, sprinkled with parsley, made his stomach queasy. He turned to Chantal, who watched the musicians, drumming her long fingers on the table to the beat.

Before he said a word, she leaned over and whispered, "You do not want them?" The question was rhetorical. She was already poking at his snails with her spoon.

"I will eat them." She switched his plate with her own empty one and in a few minutes emptied it as well.

"Where does it all go?" he whispered, placing his right hand on her slim waist, slowly enough that no else at the table would notice.

"To my heart," she said, giving him a playful sideways glance. "It's fainting with love for you and needs nourishment."

"Then I shall buy you Lafayette Gourmet." He grinned.

The champagne, the dim lights, and the sensuous blues were beginning to have an effect on him. Not to mention Chantal. He glanced at his watch to see how soon they could reasonably leave for home. Sophie was staying the night with the nanny….

An ancient Italian duke seated to Chantal's right had begun explaining, in broken French, the fine points of trombone playing. "It's very important that you do not blow with much strong force, otherwise," he put his wrinkly hands over his ears to illustrate the results, and then continued. "These instruments are very sensitive. I am never able to make my violin sing. It only cries!" Chantal listened to the man, nodding and smiling, but she squeezed Justin's hand under the table.

"The trombone can not cry when you offend it with bad playing. Like a strict maestro, it can only shout!" The Italian slapped the table and laughed.

Chantal's long body shook with her own laughter. When she turned to Justin to share her amusement with him, his heart raced. Her graciousness was contagious, and her genuine interest in the strangers sitting around him made Justin willing to be sociable. He turned to the woman seated to his left and asked, "Are you from Paris or did you come just to see Jam-buc-Blues?"

★ ★ ★

After dinner, he waved down a taxi. When they slid in, he put an arm around Chantal. She leaned her head on his shoulder. "It's almost midnight," he said, kissing back her hair.

She sat up and clapped her hands. "Ah, so the night is still young. All of that wine made me think it was quite late." She leaned over and kissed his cheek. "You are full of good ideas!"

"What idea is that?" His eyes were half closed. He scratched his jaw.

"To walk through Paris and enjoy her when she is dressed for the evening."

"A walk? If anything, I should go home and get a good night's sleep so I can be ready for the morning."

"Don't the Americans call Paris the city of lights?" she asked, arcing her arm at the grandeur of the city's skyline. "Taxi, stop! Stop here please."

The taxi swerved to the curb and stopped.

"What are you doing?" Justin asked the driver.

"Monsieur, a driver must always obey the lady. And so must a lover."

"I suppose I am out-voted," Justin said, resigned.

"*Merci beaucoup*," Chantal waved to the driver as she and Justin stepped out of the taxi, holding hands, and began to walk along the curve of the Seine.

"Are we going anywhere in particular?" Justin asked. The chill of the night felt good on his face. He breathed in the faint mist and admitted to himself that the city did have an alluring glow tonight. The sparkling silhouette of the Eiffel Tower appeared and disappeared as they strolled between the clusters of trees lining the bank.

"We must go to the middle of the Pont Neuf and make a wish," Chantal said. She snuggled up to him and slipped her arm around his waist.

"Are you sure you can walk all the way in those?" He pointed to her high-heeled shoes, which were fastened to her arched feet by two thin straps studded with faux diamonds.

"I have to walk a little to digest the fire of the music." She swung her hips as though she could still hear the band playing. "And you must walk to digest your dinner. Americans maybe do not have the enzymes to absorb horse meat so well."

"What?" He stopped walking, eyes widening.

"I said, you do not have—"

"I heard you. I ate a horse?" An image of the large piece of meat he had eaten, red and brown on the porcelain plate, arose in his mind, followed by the image of a black stallion racing across a grassy prairie. "I can't believe you let me eat horse meat."

Chantal patted his shoulder and laughed. "It's not so horrible. You seemed to be enjoying it."

"That's like telling me I've eaten my own pet." He tightened his face at the very thought.

"It wasn't a horse," she said, her voice serious.

"It wasn't," he repeated. "Let me see your face." He held her chin gently and looked into her eyes. They were at once profound and mischievous and full of love but revealed nothing pertaining to his question. She began to giggle, and he dropped his hand. "You're lying to make me feel better."

"It wasn't," she insisted, "I was just teasing you." They resumed walking, and Justin had almost decided to believe her when she made a neighing sound and burst into laughter again.

"It was," he said, pulling her to him in mock anger.

"You may never know." And then, more softly, "It will be one of the mysteries of this life."

When they reached the bridge, the moon hung wide and orange just above the buildings, leaving its color along the Seine. Chantal leaned over the stone railing, whispering some secret desire to the river. She never told him what it was.

But more a mystery to him than whether or not he ate Black Beauty was that after dancing the Tango with her in an Argentinean bar till three a.m., he was able to give a smooth presentation to the management team of Vine Industries the next morning at 7:30.

For the thousandth time, he wondered how he had ever lived before Chantal.

CHAPTER 4

Llanca, Spain
July

Sea was filling the sky. He faced the thick glass walls of what looked like a whale tank. On the other side, a group of people where thrashing for air, but the water rose and rose, stealing it. He looked for anything to break the glass. Nothing. No one on the other side could breathe.

He woke from the nightmare in a sweat.

Five a.m.

He forced himself out of bed and made a cup of coffee. He took it out to the small balcony above his back garden and stared at the sea. It laid inky blue as it should under the dawning sky. He tried to let his thoughts evaporate into that space between sea and heavens.

★ ★ ★

After dinner last night, he had walked Gloria home. The crickets were droning, and the fragrance of jasmine warmed all day in the sun hung between them in the air.

She rented a room in a residential house with friends of her family. When they neared her gate, he stopped. Light from the house brightened the street and he could see the question in her eyes. He pulled her toward him. She settled into his embrace, leaning her head against his chest. He stroked her hair and brought his hand up beneath it to the back of her neck—every nerve in him alive to the feel of her warm skin. He bent his head and kissed her—small, gentle kisses.

"I love you," he said, surprising himself. He hoped that the words hadn't sounded like a question. As he said them, they became truth, the earth he stood on.

Her arms tightened around him. She kissed her answer. Afterwards she pulled away a little and looked up at him. She did not say "I love you" back. She was Spanish, or at least half-Spanish, and he knew that she would never say this lightly. But those green eyes spoke. With a burnished hint of tears, they told him that her heart was open.

He did not want to leave her, but he still had a stray horse of anguish running around in the back of his mind. The thought took him to a bridge in Paris.

Pushing away everything but Gloria, he managed to say, "Good night."

She let him go slowly, sliding her hand down his arm, to his palm, and finally touching away the tips of his fingers.

"Good night," she said. She turned and walked through the gate. He listened to it click shut, heard her footsteps tap on the stone walk to where her door creaked open.

Then she was gone. He stood alone in the dim street, growing colder as his desire ebbed. He looked up, searching out a few familiar constellations amidst the stars. He found Orion's belt and the big dipper but had forgotten how to find the North Star with the latter. The rest of the sky was a meaningless brilliance, watched over by a sliver of moon.

He felt that now an entire corral of horses had been let loose in his heart, their hooves thudding in time with its beating.

He looked back at the empty street, irritated, wondering if he had done the right thing.

* * *

When he next noticed his coffee, it had cooled. A morning wind blew across his balcony. He exhaled until his lungs were hollow, then he took in the clean, salty air. The breath felt like a prayer.

He would go for a run. But first, he would visit Señora Pascual.

Right about now, she would have finished watering the flowers and would be taking tea with her cat.

He left his street and headed away from the port town toward the village houses beyond it, entering the cul de sac that ended in her house. The tops of her plum trees, thick and full with foliage, hung low over the stonework fence. They were shaking and rustling despite the stillness of the morning, and for a moment Justin expected to see a flock of birds rise into the sky. Then he remembered that earlier in the week she had told him she would be making jam soon. She must be picking the plums. As confirmation, he saw an arm reach through the leaves and grasp a dusty mauve fruit.

"*Bon Día, Señora,*" he called.

"Ah, you!" He heard her voice from over the fence. She met him at the gate, arms folded across her chest, shaking her head.

"What about me?" he asked, trying to recall whether he'd promised her something and forgotten to do it. The cat appeared from behind a bucket. Justin picked it up and began stroking beneath its chin.

"You took her to *La Casa Brasa*, bought her wine and then kissed her right in the street! What kind of gentleman are you? I should chase you from here with a broom."

Justin's eyes widened. "How can you know this? It has only been," he stopped to count, "ten hours, and all of them dark!"

"You cannot distract me from the point," she said. She had not yet let him inside the gate. "Are you going to do the good and honorable thing?"

"I want to," he said, setting the cat back down.

She nodded, returning to harvest the nearest tree. He joined her, pushing and stretching through the prickly branches to the plums she could not reach.

"Wanting is a strange thing. It can change from moment to moment. The will is more important," she said.

Justin didn't know how to respond to this, so he asked, "How are your grandchildren?"

"Ah, Lucia is worn out with working at the café day and night. But she is happy with the tips these tourists give her. Two nights ago a very rich man made a shocking suggestion to her and she had to keep Alberto from attacking him." Thus began the chain of local gossip. Justin made appropriate comments and questions until they had worked their way through most of her clan and the plum tree. When they had filled four large buckets, Señora Pascual said, "Enough for now. Otherwise I will have no jars left for pickling."

Justin carried the buckets to the kitchen for her. He washed the plums and helped transfer them into two large cast iron pots waiting on the stove. Then drying his hands, he excused himself. "I should start my run before the sun gets too high." Unlike the plums, the time did not seem ripe for discussing his life.

"Yes, and on Sunday you must come back to taste my first jam of the season," the Señora declared, rolling up her sleeves.

★ ★ ★

He ran his favorite route, hoping to improve his mood. It was the longest of all his regular runs—a twenty-kilometer round trip through the rocky coastal hills between Llanca and Port de la Selva.

By seven a.m., the July air was already hot and sweat began to drip down Justin's face. He wiped his forehead with the back of his hand and picked up speed. He liked to maintain a steady brisk pace for the first seven kilometers while he was still on the main road that curved along the bay.

The words the Señora had spoken remained in his mind, chafing like a shoe that raises a blister. Will or want? What was the difference? He had willed many things that had not happened and wanted many things that had. He had wanted to impress Pete Vine and climb up the corporate ladder at Vine Industries—in the blink of an eye he had become a rising star, working long hours, taking over general management of the European Headquarters at thirty-one, eating private dinners with Pete, seeking his council. Pete had become like the father he did not have.

But what had he willed? He had willed Chantal into his life.

He remembered describing her to Pete, not long after he'd begun to feel serious about the relationship. At the end of a long week of meetings during which Justin had presented plans to dramatically restructure Vine's Swiss offices, Pete and his wife Dora had invited him to spend the weekend with them in the alpine resort of Villars. On a clear September day, they convinced him to go paragliding for the first time. He ran down a slope, hooked with his instructor to a bright oblong parachute. All at once, he could no longer feel the ground beneath his feet. When he looked down, the trees were shrinking below him and the cows were turning into caramel-white dots in a green velvet ribbon of pasture.

Justin's calves tightened. The poor-night's sleep had not put him in the mood to start the morning with his ritual push-ups, sit-ups and warm-up stretches. Again, he tried to focus: 'will or want?' He could make some things happen with his will—that was true. He had done it, at least while working as a manager at Vine Industries. Then again, the world around him did not stay static and had a way of escaping from one's will. It had a dynamism and force of its own.

He had learned this the hard way. So why did will even matter?

CHAPTER 5

Paris, France
August 14th, the previous year

Justin was worried. The new project was crashing. And not just the project—things were not going well in any sector of Vine Industries.

He picked up the restaurant bill from last night's dinner with Pete. Though Pete kept his headquarters in California, he liked to visit a few of his European offices and factories whenever he came through. Justin, being top manager, had accompanied him to the sites during the past week. Last night they finished with a fine meal overlooking the Seine, discussing what they had seen and what they were planning for the meeting.

Pete and Dora had invited twelve of the top managers and their families to the company's annual meeting—in Malta. The charter flight for the Vines and Justin's family had departed at ten this morning. Justin was not on board.

His secretary, Eva, had called him as he had been helping Chantal and Sophie out onto the runway. A Russian diplomat he had been trying to contact for ages happened to be in Paris that morning and was willing to have an impromptu meeting. Justin had assisted everyone into the plane, waved good-bye, and taken a car back into the city. Eva had already booked a commercial flight so that he could join them the next morning.

Unfortunately, the diplomat hadn't been worth the wait or delay.

Justin sighed, wishing he were seated next to Chantal, looking through the oval airplane window over the South of France.

★ ★ ★

Later that afternoon, Justin saw the Russian to his hotel and returned to his office to pick up his jacket and some papers and close down his computer. On the way home, he stopped into a jeweler's studio around the corner from his office building.

Chantal had brought Sophie to visit him at work yesterday, and they had all headed out for lunch. As they walked past store fronts, Chantal explained that Sophie had been throwing everything out of the suitcases as she packed them. To avoid hysterics, they had come to see Daddy—armed with several cookies.

"You say these are the 'terrible two's', no?" Chantal had asked, brushing Sophie's crumb-covered red mouth with equal parts love and exasperation.

Justin had leaned over to take the squirming two-year-old in question from his wife's arms, kissing them both in the process. "And you are terrific at handling them so well," he had assured her.

Arms finally free, Chantal had wasted no time using them to exclaim over items in shop windows. She had stopped at the jeweler's and taken a deep breath at a carved jade ring. She reached over toward Justin for Sophie's fat little hand and pointed it playfully at the window. "Sophie, look at the pretty green. Isn't that pretty?"

Justin had smiled as they walked down to a favorite open-air café.

Now, he emerged from the shop and stood under its azure awning with a wrapped purchase. His cell phone rang just as he started trying to tuck the box into his attaché case. He almost did not bother to flip open the phone. But, finally getting box and cell where they needed to be, he answered, "Justin Collins speaking."

And there on the sidewalk, with the rich orange light of late summer evening dusting the trees in gold, Justin's world went black.

* * *

Fragments of the woman's words rolled back and forth through his head. *The aviation authority is so sorry to inform you.* He vaguely remembered walking through streets he did not recognize. *Somewhere between France and Malta.*

Street after street, a continuous blur of faces bobbed past him. Every woman with pale blond hair wore Chantal's face. Every toddler turned to him with the face of Sophie. *Something went wrong with chartered jet A776-507. It went down in the Mediterranean.*

On the Rue St.-Antoine, he simply stood still in the middle of the sidewalk, distantly holding on to his attaché, his other arm limp at this side. *Only an airplane seat, a doll and an oil slick on the water's surface.*

Moving would have meant going forward without them, would have meant focusing on a world without them, and he could do neither. When he looked up, it was dark, and the streetlights didn't seem to be doing anything about it. The night rose in him and filled his soul.

There were no survivors.

CHAPTER 6

January

He was staring off into nothing again. If he didn't watch himself, he could lose hours—coming to his senses in freezing bath water, with petrified charred potatoes in the oven, with the phone in his hand long after a call had ended.

He only answered calls because of Vine Industries. Since Pete and Dora's deaths, the business had been sold off, and its Paris offices were being dismantled. He had to get his head together enough now and then to answer questions.

The phone rang.

"Mr. Collins? This is Eva." His secretary.

"Yes?" He didn't have the energy to be polite.

"I'm just calling to let you know that they have started clearing out the offices. Movers are coming for the furniture tomorrow."

He didn't see why she was calling. He knew this.

Sounds of banging and voices came through the line along with muffled curses in French. It sounded like men were dragging a filing cabinet.

Eva continued, speaking slowly, "I thought you might stop by and see if you've left anything. Anything in your desk, on the *walls….*" She stopped to let the word sink in.

Oh, God, he thought, reverently. It was still hanging on the wall.

He thanked Eva and hung up, actually remembering to return his phone to its cradle.

* * *

The next day it started raining just as movers loaded a large, flat package, wrapped thickly with brown paper, into a rented storage unit on the edge of Paris.

Justin had never stolen anything in his life. He was surprised that he felt no twinge of guilt as he watched them set the painting down. He was sure that Pete Vine would not have objected.

The mother-and-child painting had hung behind Eva's desk in the offices' reception room. Chantal had signed it with her artist's name, her maiden name—Chevalier. And though it technically belonged to Vine Industries, he had the feeling no one would miss it. And he knew with absolute certainly that no one needed it as much as he did.

He thanked the movers and signed their bill, turning from them to the small unit.

Its walls were lined with other wrapped paintings of similar shapes and heights from their apartment. Half a dozen boxes stood next to them. He went over to a small square one and pulled off the tape. Inside was a doll. Though water- and oil-stained, it still closed its eyes when lying down and opened them when held upright. Justin picked it up and looked into the plastic pupils, then held the doll against his chest. It smelled of seawater and damp.

★ ★ ★

He left five dead plants and all the furniture in the Paris apartment, not caring if the landlord charged him for their removal.

He took a taxi to the station and bought a one-way ticket to Barcelona. The poster behind the saleslady made it look as good a place as any. He considered visiting the Vine Industries factory in Sant Cugat near Barcelona. He had friends there. The factory had been purchased by Unipac, the electronics conglomerate based in the Silicon Valley. After the buy out, Unipac had put a young manager in place named Hank Morgan and Justin heard good things about him. But on second thought, he knew that visiting the factory would only increase the pain he was feeling.

As his train reached the south of France, Justin began to glimpse hints of a stormy sea. Crossing into Spain, the sea filled more and more of his window. He watched it over jagged coastline that began to spread into hills and small mountains.

He felt called by the water and realized he could not stay away. His wife and daughter were at the bottom of it somewhere.

His train changed in Port Bou. There, the size of the Spanish tracks was different from the French. The Paris train he had been riding headed back to France, and he had a bit of time before his express train headed south to Barcelona.

Yet the express did not stop by the coastal towns. The commuter did. He rarely changed his plans.

He checked the commuter schedule and saw he had over half an hour to kill before it came. Decision made. He walked into the cold, deserted town and found the first café that was open, a place called Art in Café.

After sitting down, Justin ordered an espresso and stared at the stone walls and black-and-white floors. He watched the waiter step behind the counter and grind some coffee beans. A pretty, blue-eyed woman approached him and whispered in his ear. They laughed and put their arms around each other.

Justin could not take his eyes off her as he thought of Chantal. He barely tasted the heady caffeine in its small cup and vaguely remembered that he had a train to catch. To where, he was not even sure.

On the slower train, he watched the sea getting closer and closer. By the time he reached the coastal town of Llanca, he only hesitated a moment before pulling his suitcase from the overhead shelf and getting off. He left his luggage in a station locker and headed for the gray beach.

A bitter, cold wind rolled at him, but he did not feel the heavy, wet air on his bare head and hands. He had to walk to the sea.

It started to rain hard, soaking him as he made his way to the shallow waves. He would have kept going, but the water did not let him in. It would not let him leave, either.

He stood facing that cold, blue fate.

CHAPTER 7

Llanca, Spain
January

How long was it that he stood there? He was soaked and chilled to the bone. Shaking with cold, he turned back to the village in search of drying warmth.

At the first open café, he made straight for the heater, oblivious to stares from the few patrons inside.

Hands numb, he alternated between holding his cup of coffee in one hand and placing the other as close to the heating element as possible. It was so old that its metal frame buzzed and vibrated.

The strong black coffee stirred some sense of survival in him. He needed to find a place to spend the night.

When the waiter passed, Justin asked in French, *"Excusez-moi monsieur. Est-ce que vous savez s'il y un hôtel à Llanca qui est ouvert? Je cherche une chambre pour la nuit."* The man shook his head, indicating that he did not speak French, but he pointed to a group of five men seated at a round table near the door drinking beer. Justin shrugged his shoulders, not in the mood to interrupt a party of strangers, and bent back over the heater.

A moment later, he noticed the waiter had approached the group. One of them, a stocky muscular man with black curly hair and deep brown eyes came over to his table. He stood straight, much like a soldier, but wore authority rather than submission on his rugged face. His lips turned up slightly into the beginnings of a smile as he asked in careful English, "Do you come from England?"

"No. I'm American." Justin stood up to shake hands. He realized the man was tall, just under his own six foot four inches.

The man took his hand, but the smile receded and the man's face became stiff. He stepped back to look Justin up and down. He said, "We do not have many American visitors in Llanca. Most go to Barcelona or Madrid."

Justin sat down again to be nearer the heater but gestured for the man to have a seat. "I am on my way to Barcelona," he replied. "I only need a room for the night."

"Most of the large hotels are closed in winter. I can have one of my friends take you to a small guest house if you like." The man remained standing, looking down at him. Justin felt strange, being examined so openly, and he ran his fingers through his damp hair, smoothing it back. The man continued abruptly, "You look like you need help. They will take care of you."

"What do you mean?" Justin felt his body stiffen. The man's statement, obvious though it was, made Justin see himself as others had over the last months: a broken man.

"Hombre, you look like a man who needs care," the man replied, and without further comment, he called to one of his friends at the round table, "Pascual!" He began speaking in Catalan, a Latin language influenced by Italian, Spanish and French that Justin did not know. Pascual stood up and approached Justin's table. He was at least six inches shorter than the first man but muscular as well. He wore a jacket with yellow, red and blue colors that Justin recognized as belonging to the Football Club of Barcelona. Pascual conferred with the bigger man, then waved to the group at the table, lifted Justin's

pack and said "*Venez.*"

Justin finished his coffee in one swift gulp and followed Pascual out of the café. They turned in and out of so many small streets that Justin had no sense of where he was. At last they stopped in front of a wide three-story house at the end of a cul de sac surrounded by a courtyard and a garden full of well-pruned fruit trees. "*La casa de mi madre.*" Pascual said, enunciating and slowing his Spanish for Justin's sake.

As he spoke, he knocked at the front door, calling "*Mama, tengo alguien, un American, por la cuarto.*"

The door swung open to reveal a short, round Catalan lady in a conservative black dress, wearing her gray-black hair pulled tightly back. She smiled at Justin and said in English, "Welcome."

Pascual left him at the door and Señora Pascual led him up to a modest but tidy room on the third floor. Aside from the twin bed and a plain wooden writing table, the room had a wide cushioned chair in which one could sit and stare out across the tile rooftops of Llanca into the village square. The walls were bright yellow, and a hand-made quilt covered the bed. He put his bag down, nodding and smiling to the Señora.

She began speaking, very rapidly, in a mixture of French, Catalan and Spanish. Though Justin could not quite work out all of what she said, he understood that after he put on some dry clothes she wanted him to come back downstairs.

After obeying, he found himself in a warm stone kitchen with a fire blazing in the fireplace. Señora Pascual smiled as she made him sit near it. She promptly presented him with a pastry he did not recognize and a glass of tea to which she'd added a good deal of strong alcohol. He stared into the crackling orange flames, eating and drinking. He had eaten nothing that day.

The house was old enough that Justin guessed the fireplace must have been used for cooking once. Now, Señora Pascual stood at a gas stove frying pieces of fish and sprinkling them with various spices. She talked all the while, and from the bits and phrases of language he could identify, Justin gathered she was a widow, that her husband had left her this home, and that her grandchildren visited her often—she hoped he didn't mind. He felt he wouldn't mind anything, as long as he was warm, but he knew his chill was coming from inside and the fire could only warm a part of him.

Yet that night, he slept more soundly than he had since he had heard of the crash.

✳ ✳ ✳

In the morning, quite early, he showered, shaved and dressed. He tiptoed down the stairs, intending to go out on a walk and orient himself as to the layout of the town. To his surprise, Señora Pascual was seated on a plastic stool outside the front door, sipping tea and petting a very large white tomcat. She told him a storm was headed up the coast and that he should eat his breakfast quickly if he planned to see the town before it began to rain.

"Is there a place to find breakfast this early?" he asked, mixing the few Spanish words he knew together with his French.

"Here you eat your breakfast," she said in English. She stood and let the cat fall to the ground. It immediately began rubbing itself up against her legs and mewing. She shooed it away with several claps of her hands, then directed Justin to the kitchen again. She lay breakfast before him—an omelet, fresh bread, homemade plum jam and thick black coffee. He had had so little appetite for so long that he was surprised to find he'd cleared his plate.

"A man in trouble can no forget to eat," she admonished him, as if reading his mind. "Then the heart *and* body get sick." He could do nothing but agree with her, happily full in her warm kitchen.

He had a second cup of coffee listening to the Señora's sing-song chatter. He was glad not to feel the loneliness of a boarder in a hotel—a feeling he had known well for a long time as a businessman. Rather, he felt like the Señora's long lost relative. He reached for more bread and jam.

✳ ✳ ✳

Near the end of his second week in Llanca, as he was walking through the streets, finally getting his bearings, he ran into the man who had introduced him to Pascual in the café.

The man spoke first. "I thought you said you needed a room for one night. Yet, you are still here. You are liking Señora Pascual's cooking?"

"You were right," Justin replied. "It's a good place."

The man said, "You look much better now." Then, without another word, he turned and walked down a side street, leaving Justin staring after him.

That evening, in the kitchen, Justin asked Señora Pascual, "Do you know the man who sent me to your place? The one who introduced me to your son and told him to bring me here?"

The Señora did not answer, so Justin continued, "He was a large Spanish man, muscular, with black hair and deep brown eyes."

For the first time the Señora seemed at a loss for words. She coughed, and then she spoke. "Yes, I know the man."

"Well, who is he? What does he do?" Justin asked.

She looked at Justin, her expression serious, and said, "He will let you know in his time, if he wants to. But he would not like to be known as Spanish. He is Catalan." At that she walked away.

CHAPTER 8

Toward the end of winter, a storm rolled through Llanca, similar to the one that had brought Justin there. He returned to the boarding house soaked. Out for a walk, he had been caught in the sudden downpour and wind. He made straight for the kitchen fireplace. The Señora cleared her throat and offered him a drink.

"It's a very special drink," she said, lowering her voice as if she were sharing a secret. "It's good after a walk in the bad weather."

She kept up a regular flow of chatter whenever they were together. He had plenty of practice at sorting out her sentences. "Is it a Llanca specialty?" he asked.

"It's a specialty of the Pascual family. My husband's grandfather taught his father to make it, and his father taught him." She handed him a fragile, port-style glass. Her smile widened as he took a sip.

The dense fire of the alcohol burned his mouth and throat. He began to cough and thumped his sternum a few times with his fist. "Strong," he gasped. The intense flavor of fruit remained as an aftertaste on his tongue. He felt a warmth emanate out from his stomach into his limbs. "But delicious."

"Yes," she said, "it's a man's drink, but I like it." She lifted a glass to her lips, threw her head back and emptied it in one gulp. Then she sighed and looked at him. She said, "Go ahead!"

He felt that to protect his dignity, he had no choice but to do the same. He swallowed the remainder of his drink. His throat tightened as he fought to stifle another round of coughing. He put his glass down on the table, frowning slightly as she refilled it but not her own. She gestured for him to take a seat by the fire and then pulled a chair over so she could join him.

A crash of thunder brought the cat running into the kitchen where it stretched out in front of them, basking in the firelight. Justin whistled and patted his knee to encourage the cat to jump in his lap but it began licking its front paw.

The Señora picked up a ball of blue yarn and threw it to Justin. "For your lap," she laughed. "Keep the tension for me." She began clicking away with her knitting needles, working on what looked to be a sweater.

"Family tradition," she said. "It's very important. My son can also make this drink. And when he has a son, that son will make it, too." Justin took a sip from his glass as the Señora continued, "Your family must have traditions. No?"

"No."

"Your *madre*, she doesn't make a jam or a pickle she learned from her *madre*?"

"No." He shifted in his seat and stared into the fireplace. The coals glowed and flickered under two flaming logs.

"What does she do?" The Señora had stopped moving the needles and sounded distressed at the thought of a woman who did not know how to preserve anything.

"Nothing." Justin said, and since he knew she would ask, he added, "She's dead."

"And your papa is all alone in America?"

Justin finished his drink quickly and held out his glass to her. She refilled it. She looked at him and said, "I see. He is dead too."

"Yes," Justin said.

She put down her knitting and crossed herself. "In the name of the Father, the Son and the Holy Ghost. God give their souls peace."

"No grandparents either," Justin added abruptly, feeling he ought to cut to the chase. He didn't intend to be rude to the Señora. She had made Llanca a refuge for him, and until now, she had never asked him any personal questions. She had a certain amount of protective concern for him—the mysterious boarder who came to her house wet and cold, the boarder she had been feeding with hearty and elaborate meals for a month.

Still, he didn't particularly like conversations about family. Redundant pity could get on anyone's nerves. So far, though, the Señora's responses had been matter-of-fact. At least the strong alcohol made the process tolerable.

"And you are living and working in France?" the Señora asked, her tone casual as she unraveled a bit of the sweater and then resumed knitting.

He downed his third shot and remained silent, listening to the heavy clatter of rain against the windowpane. The wind began to blow in loud moaning gusts, rattling the kitchen shutters, banging them against the outside wall of the house. "I'll go out and shut those," Justin said, starting to get up from his chair.

"No. The windows can bear this wind. The storm is a small one." The Señora rose from her chair, stirred the fire and added another log. Before she sat again, she filled his glass, and her own.

Justin held his glass up to the firelight, moving it in small circles. The thick ruby liqueur was almost opaque. "It looks like blood," he said.

"My husband," the Señora said, "was a fisherman. He lived on the sea. I knew he loved this sea. She was like another woman, beautiful and overpowering. Sometimes I felt jealous and when he came home late from fishing, I wouldn't speak to him. But I thought one day about how his father had been a fisherman, and his father's father. He could not be anything other than a fisherman. And he could not resist the sea. I no longer felt angry with him, and when he came home late, I welcomed him and smiled and fed him a good dinner. I told him that if one day the sea disappeared, I knew he would disappear, too. After that we were very happy. We had three children. Then one day he did not come home. The sea had her own jealousies. She grew stormy in her anger. She did not like him leaving her every day. So she pulled him down to her bosom and smothered him."

"I'm sorry," Justin said, his own loss rising like bile in his throat.

"You see," she said, not acknowledging the interruption, "my husband had two beautiful lovers. Myself and the sea. He found life in them both. They both seemed tame to him. And both of them could have consumed him in their rage. But he loved them both, so he did not know it. One of them loved him best and though he knew it, he stayed a fisherman."

Justin was not sure what point she was making here. But he understood the relationship between the fisherman and the sea—on several levels.

He decided to answer her earlier question. "I did work in France for an international American company. But its owner died. After that, the whole thing fell apart."

"Was it such a bad company that it should not survive the loss of the owner?" Señora Pascual asked, at ease with his sudden confession.

Her incisive question surprised Justin. While he knew she was not a learned woman, and her philosophizing struck him as somewhat abstruse, this was a question any level headed investor would have asked. "That is something I could never understand." That and the loss that had kept him from focusing on the company as it plummeted. "It kept its books well, its factories produced excellent medical and electronic equipment, its research and development branch was the envy of its competitors, but when the owner died, the investors pulled away." Justin wanted to avoid mentioning Pete Vine's name. He wanted to avoid that emotion too.

"They didn't trust the people who were left to run it?"

She tugged at the yarn, and Justin realized he'd forgotten to keep unraveling the ball.

"It felt to me like some outside force was working against us. We lost support in the stock market. Then the board of directors appointed an interim management team and when they came, the real trouble started. This team let themselves be controlled by a group of minority shareholders who saw the opportunity for a lot of profit in the divestiture of the company. Some board members also made a lot of profit."

He looked at the Señora, his eyes bright. She kept her head bent, but peered up at him sheepishly and grinned. "What?" he said, irritated by her apparent amusement.

"Señor Justin, you are using French business words I do not understand. You must explain more clearly."

"I'm sorry," he sighed. "Well, you understand newspapers and magazines, right?"

She nodded.

"The newspapers and magazines were filled with false stories about poor accounting, potential law suits and loss of buyers for our goods. Then, many stockholders sold their shares in our company. The new managing team, the temporary CEO and a few members of the board of directors used their power to sell much of our company to other companies called 'asset-strippers.'"

"I don't understand these asset strippers," she stated.

He replied, "Oh, you might say they are companies that buy other companies at a cheap price when the company for sale is in a weak position. Then the new owners sell the assets at an inflated price and they make a lot of money. The problem is they don't really think about the people in the company, or about the long-term health of the company. But, one of the strange things in our case was that some companies bought pieces of Vine Industries where it didn't make sense."

Señora Pascual listened, knitting.

Justin continued. "Even some unheard-of companies came like sharks to eat the dying fish." He liked this metaphor. The picture seemed more than accurate to him and he knew that the Señora would not fail to understand it. "Some companies like EuroVinco and GauLux bought many pieces of Vine Industries ."

"Why did they buy them then?"

"I have no idea." Justin shrugged.

Another explosion of thunder shook the house, and the cat jumped up and scrambled under Justin's chair.

"It sounds like the storm is right over our heads," Justin said.

"It's nothing," the Señora insisted. "Did this selling of the company end your work?"

"No. Another U.S. company called Unipac became involved in the situation. Unipac did some good things for us. They paid a fair price for some of Vine's manufacturing plants and other offices, mostly in North America. They bought as many of our company's pieces as possible to help keep things together, but only ended up owning one factory near Barcelona. Another company, EuroVinco, bought many of our factories and sales offices in Europe. The founder of Unipac had been a good friend with the founder of my own company. That is why he made such an effort to bring things to a positive end for us. In any case, I could have continued working, but the new managers from EuroVinco wanted to reorganize everything and I was offered a good severance package. I was glad to take it."

"So you are now a charming drifter planning to rob me?" the Señora asked, laughing.

"Is that what you thought?" Justin looked away from the fire to her, surprised.

"No. When my son brought you here I knew I could trust you. The gossiping old ladies in Llanca are never tired of creating a rumor, though, and they have been guessing about you. One of them warned me you might slit my throat in the night."

"Slit your throat! Do I look like the kind of person who would slit a woman's throat?" Justin asked, genuinely amused.

"Oh, not at all. My friends say you are very handsome and polite and that you no bother anyone," the Señora protested. "They wonder, mostly, why you staying in Llanca."

Justin guessed that this last comment was actually a question, which he was welcome to answer or ignore as he pleased. "Señora," he said, for he had been thinking it during their conversation, "I am a businessman who lost his business and something else even more important. I am like your fisherman who lost his sea. Without a sea, what am I?"

CHAPTER 9

Mid-March

This was getting ridiculous. The tiny grocer's wife was pumping her arms up and down, trying—Justin could only guess—to demonstrate how to pound the bottom off the massive head of lettuce he had picked up. His questioning lift of it towards her had been to find out how much it cost. It looked like he was getting salad prep lessons.

What he needed were Spanish lessons. He gave up and decided to shop tomorrow. He swiped at the hair in his face that had grown past his ears. It seemed he also needed a haircut.

A few narrow streets back, he had noticed a barbershop. Returning there, he paused under a small yellow sign that read, 'Eusebi, Coiffure.' Below it, an open doorframe was curtained off with a stained yellow cloth.

Justin stepped inside to another world. The barbershop was the complete antithesis of the clean, plastic salons that he had found in Paris or New York. This was no place for pretty boys.

His eyes took a few moments to adjust to the dim interior. The barber motioned with his hand for Justin to sit down in the barber chair and, without asking what style, he set to cutting. Justin looked around the large room, careful to keep his head still. On the walls hung numerous posters of famous Spanish football teams, many of F.C. Barcelona, the team most Catalans supported. Justin also noticed a row of framed photographs depicting children's football teams. When he looked closely, he recognized the barber standing proudly in coach position beside the teammates.

In between the football things hung long-expired calendars of nude women. On another wall Justin saw a diploma from the 'Institute des Coiffures de Paris' and under it an award given at a hair-stylist convention in Barcelona. Well, at least he did not have to worry about getting sheared.

In the back corner of the room, two cracked leather couches faced each other at an angle in front of an old television set stacked with sports magazines and newspapers.

Eusebi reached for a different comb from a small shelf in front of Justin. Dust had settled on all of the bottles of hair spray, powders and perfumes, papers, and a small statue of the Virgin Mary. At least a week's worth of hair lay under her pensive eyes on the floor.

A man walked into the shop, sat down and talked with Eusebi for a couple of minutes, then left. Another went to the couch with a magazine, flipped through it, then left the shop without saying a word.

Justin was fascinated by this inner sanctum. And though none of the dingy objects in the room would seem to suggest it, he had the indefinable sense that this was a place of honor.

Justin hadn't noticed a dark wooden door in the back of the shop. It suddenly opened and light shot into the room as a man walked through the door. Once again, Justin was looking at the man he had met his first day in Llanca—the large, muscular man with dark eyes.

He saw Justin in the barber's chair and smiled. "*Hombre,*" he said. "You have come to a good place. Eusebi is the best."

The barber seemed to understand and he smiled, setting down his scissors. He went to the counter, picked up a pack of cigarettes and lit one.

Justin said, "I thought it was about time. People would start saying I'm a hippy from California."

"You come from California?"

"Yes, I grew up there."

"It's a good place. Many people speak Spanish there."

"I know. I had some Spanish in high school," Justin said, almost apologetically, knowing he could only speak a few phrases.

"You want to learn Spanish?" the man asked. "Catalan is better."

"First, I would like to learn Spanish and—why not Catalan after that."

"I can arrange for you to learn Spanish," said the man, "then I can arrange for you to learn Catalan."

Justin would be glad to do something with his time. And to communicate at the market. "So you know someone who would want to teach me?

"My friend Antonio works at the bank. Perhaps he could find somebody. Can you meet me at the Pacu-Pacu bar this evening? Nine o'clock."

"Yes, thank you. I will be there at nine." He paused a second. "Could I ask you a question? How did you learn English?"

The man laughed and said, "I learned it when I was in the French Foreign Legion. We were many nationalities, and I had the chance to learn English and of course French."

"Why did you join the French Foreign Legion?" Justin asked.

"That's another story," the man replied. End of discussion.

Not wanting the conversation to finish on this abrupt note, Justin added, "By the way, my name is Justin Collins."

"I know."

Justin should not have been surprised. "What is your name?" he had to ask.

"Jordi," the man replied, "Jordi Pujols. Nine o'clock at the Pacu-Pacu bar," he said, holding up the old yellow curtain and walking out the door.

Justin sat there waiting for a few minutes while Eusebi the barber finished his cigarette. When the haircut started again he asked him in French who Jordi was.

"*Amigo*," the barber answered and continued to cut his hair without saying anything more.

That evening Justin arrived at nine at the Pacu-Pacu bar. It was a locals' place near the port. When Justin walked in, a man tapped him on the shoulder. "Señor, my name is Antonio. My friend Jordi said you want to learn Spanish. A trainee from my bank is willing to give you lessons. The trainee will be here soon to meet you."

Antonio took a seat and Justin ordered two beers. They waited together for half an hour, getting into a discussion about banking and the economy. Justin noticed Antonio's surprise at how much 'the American' knew about these things.

At nine thirty Antonio looked up. "There she is. There is the trainee."

Justin turned and his heart jumped. Coming toward them was the green-eyed young woman he had watched sleeping on the train two weeks ago. He suddenly felt self-conscious about having followed her home. She went over to Antonio. Justin stood up to meet her, and Antonio made the introductions. "Mr. Justin Collins, this is Gloria Montalvo-Butler. She may give you Spanish lessons."

She held out her hand. Justin shook it and said, 'I'm pleased to meet you.

"And I you," she replied.

Two pairs of green eyes held and locked of their own will.

Justin and Gloria decided to meet twice a week for Spanish lessons. Starting the following day.

CHAPTER 10

April—June

Gloria had cooked dinner at his house. Afterwards, they worked on improving Justin's slowly growing Spanish vocabulary.

An hour passed. Justin was mangling a string of words that Gloria patiently repeated for him. He shook his head, saying what he thought was, "I am embarrassed."

Gloria burst into a fit of giggles, gasping, "And who's the lucky mother?"

Justin's face contracted in puzzlement.

She took his hand, explaining, "*Embarazada* means 'pregnant,' not 'embarrassed.'"

Justin slapped the heel of his hand to his forehead.

Gloria went on, "There is a funny story about that. An American company that manufactures ballpoint pens wanted to advertise a new pen in Mexico. The ads were supposed to say, "It won't leak in your pocket and embarrass you."

"Let me guess," Justin interrupted. "They translated: 'It won't leak in your pocket and make you pregnant.'" He laughed with her.

"Well," he said, "I guess language lessons are also healthy lessons in humility. How about a walk? I think I've 'impregnated' myself enough for today, don't you?"

★ ★ ★

He helped her into her jacket and then put on his own. She smiled, pulling out his jacket collar that had turned under.

They stepped out into the brisk air. A biting breeze rose and fell across them. From the hilltop where his house was situated, they could see the whole of Llanca and the bright fishing boats floating in the bay.

"Sometimes, on spring days like this, I feel like the bank is a prison and I can hardly concentrate on my work. I want to be outside breathing the air." Gloria bent to pick a small white stone. She wiped the dust from it and put it in her pocket.

He felt encouraged by her peaceful mood and her simple comfortable gestures. He could not help saying, "Maybe one day we can have a picnic after work. By the bay."

"I think when it's warmer, that would be perfect," she said. "When I was growing up, we had a custom of going on a picnic every warm Saturday. Even some cold Saturdays we went. Papa was from Scotland and the cold never bothered him."

"Did the cold bother you?" Justin asked.

"Yes, I think I inherited my mama's Spanish blood. In Scotland, I have heard, there is very little sun." She shivered at the thought.

"So your father is Scottish." They had not yet spoken to each other of family and though Justin hated the topic, he felt compelled to satisfy his curiosity about this lovely woman: her life, her interests, her loyalties.

"Yes. He came to Barcelona to teach at University."

"And is your mother a Barcelona native?"

"Yes and no. She grew up in Barcelona, but in Europe we tend to identify with our family origins. My mother's ancestors several generations back were actually from Andalusia, where they were very poor, so they moved to the north for work. It's good that they did. A fortunate misfortune, as they say. Otherwise, my mother would never have met my father."

"And you might not be here. And we might not be speaking."

"How strange it is that you say so." Gloria stopped to watch a brown bird rustling in the scrub. "Over the weekend, my mama was telling us of a Catalan poet who writes about these things. He calls them 'blue fate.'"

"I don't like the idea of fate," Justin said, but was unnerved, remembering his first night in Llanca, standing in front of the sea.

"Why not?"

The bird hopped out of sight and they resumed walking. "I don't think there's enough meaning in this world for fate or destiny," he answered.

"But have you never met people whom you knew you were destined to meet?"

"I have." Justin's hands went cold.

Gloria saw a change in his expression. She looked away. "I am sorry. I reminded you of a pain."

He forced himself to mention it, for the first time. "It is still with me. One day it will go away."

Gloria did not reply. They continued across the hillside trying to pay attention to the spring foliage. Thin leaves sprouted up bright green between the pale rocks. Puddles from the recent rain lay in their path. While they were stepping over a wide patch of muddy ground, Gloria slipped, startling him.

He caught her around the waist and held her for a few seconds, making sure she had regained her balance.

She slid out of his grasp and straightened her jacket, which had bunched upward and revealed her smooth brown abdomen.

Her beauty alarmed him. He stared at her, troubled.

"I'm fine," she said.

"That's not it." He paused, it was now or never. "Gloria, I need to tell you something."

* * *

They walked down the port road, approaching the bay at an oblique angle. The sun left the sky and they walked closer together to keep warm.

"It's good to remember the dead, and to honor them," Gloria said, after he told her of Chantal. Of Sophie.

They stopped at a rocky outcropping and faced the water as it pulsed toward them.

"Is this what drew you to live here—the sea?" Gloria asked.

"Yes," Justin said, surprised at her insight.

"Yet you do not think it is a good fate that brought you here?"

Justin did not answer. He simply reached for her hand, letting the wind lift their hair and the edges of their clothing. Justin did not notice the cold. But finally, Gloria pulled at his hand, bringing him to face her. "I know another warm place where we can sit."

⋆ ⋆ ⋆

They reached the empty plaza at the center of town where all was dark except for several second and third story windows in the surrounding buildings. Gloria led him to the pale stone front of the Catholic church.

The sound of the door creaking on its hinges made him feel that he ought to whisper. As he entered, he could smell traces of incense from the evening mass. Muted lamps lined a narrow stone aisle, and centered at the head of the aisle stood an altar. A gold chalice rested on it between two tall, unlit candles. In a corner to the right of the altar a life-sized statue of the virgin watched from her semi-circular niche. In front of her, on a wooden table, burned a circle of small candles.

"I hope you do not mind that I brought you here," she said.

"It feels strange," Justin said, looking up at the arched ceiling. Though it was warmer than outside, the place seemed chilled to him. "I haven't been to a church, well, not since Chantal wanted Sophie to be christened."

"Was Chantal Catholic?" Gloria asked.

"She was Protestant, from French Huguenot origins. She started to go to a Protestant church in Paris after we were married. She liked it—even went to Mass sometimes at Notre Dame Cathedral. Around our home she often sang hymns in French."

"My father is Anglican, but my mother is a Catholic, and she taught me that it's good to pray for the souls of the dead." Gloria hesitated, and then asked very softly, "Would you mind if I prayed for Chantal and Sophie?"

Justin was too exhausted by his confession to care. But when Gloria approached the niche and lit two candles, he wondered how many before them had burned away to nothing. He closed his eyes—purely from exhaustion—and had a fleeting vision of a tall Señor with piercing eyes.

⋆ ⋆ ⋆

Almost two months into Spanish lessons, and Justin's head was swimming with Spanish Grammar. He had to admit that the motivation for learning this language came not from the grand and varied country of Spain herself, but from one of her curvaceous countrywomen.

He closed his books and decided to go for a real swim.

He walked to the port road and hitched a ride toward Port de la Selva. A fisherman he knew drove him the final three kilometers to the long stretch of beach just before the village. When the man drove off, Justin stripped to his shorts. He left his clothes in a pile on the sand, waded until he was chest deep, and then dove under the swells. He swam with long powerful strokes to a point in the middle of the bay, several hundred meters from shore. There he stopped to tread water and catch his breath.

Rising from the western hills, the monastery of Sant Pere de Rhodes looked back at him from the top of its small mountain. To the southwest, Port de la Selva sprawled in a cream, beige and white patchwork of houses and shops. At his immediate left, the main docks stood empty of fishing boats. They were all out at sea.

He swam slowly back toward shore. He felt his muscles, taut and strong under his skin. Six months of running and exercise had put him in the best shape he had been in for a long time—as good, if not better, than when he was at UCLA.

He was fortunate to have stepped off the train in Llanca, to have met Señora Pascual. And, whether it was fate or accident or some other force at play, he was doubly fortunate to have met a woman like Gloria. All that fate and fortune stuff—it kept coming at him.

He waded out of the sea and sat on the sand for some minutes while the water evaporated from his long body.

The past had kept him from seeing the present as it was.

"What do I really want?" he asked aloud.

But he knew his answer.

CHAPTER 11

Llanca, Spain
July

Señora Pascual had told him yesterday that if he kept up all this running, he'd run himself into nothing. This she had emphasized by heaving onto his plate a massive portion of lamb.

Even though he had moved out of her boarding house into his own place overlooking Llanca's port, the Señora was not convinced that he could feed himself. If he was not eating with Gloria—and the Señora would know—she expected him at her table.

Justin laughed as he ran. He was more of the opinion that he needed to run *because* of her cooking.

Justin left the dirt path he was on and followed a winding course along the side of the hill, his laughter leaving him. Into its place crept a soft and haunting melancholy, reminding him that it still rested in his heart.

He came to a stop, taking in the summer growth around him. Soft pink wildflowers shaped like bottlebrushes sprang up between the rocks. He picked two and held them gently in his cupped hand as he climbed over the rough terrain.

He slowly rounded the hillside until he came to a rock ledge that jutted out about a meter above the sea. The ledge was worn smooth into a hard seat large enough for two. Likely a rendezvous point for lovers. He stepped out onto the flat stone surface and dropped the two flowers into the sea. A small wave caught and lifted them toward the rocks. He squatted and looked into the water, trying to regain sight of them. After a moment, he spotted them in the bubbles and foam. The fact that they had somehow stayed together comforted him. He slid down into a sitting position, letting his legs hang over the water. He watched the flowers drift.

Then he looked up at the hot sky and whispered, "Why?"

Gloria prayed with an air of assurance that someone was listening. The night he had stood with her in Llanca's Catholic church, she had begun her prayer with a soft, "*Señor.*" He had felt for a split second that God could be a Spaniard, standing right in front of him.

Waves crashed against the rocks below him, sending up a cold spray which soaked his tired legs. He shuddered at the thought of Chantal and Sophie beneath the dark blue sea, empty of all breath.

"I didn't even get to say good bye to you," he called after the flowers, now swallowed under foam.

More softly, he said, "I'm so sorry I let you die alone." Had this also been plaguing him—that he felt he should have gone down with them? He tried to release his guilt and pain with the flowers.

This would be his final goodbye. Abruptly, he stood up. *A grieving heart lives with memories,* Gloria had said.

"Good bye, *ma cherie.* Good bye, petite Sophie," and turned away from the water toward Port de la Selva.

★ ★ ★

Nine time zones away, two men sat down at a linen-covered corner table at the Ritz-Carlton. A musician played *"Georgia on my mind"* on a grand piano opposite them.

One of the men asked, "You ever been here before?"

"No, I don't know San Francisco very well, but with these monthly trips I'm discovering more and more of the city."

"You'll like the food in here."

The two men quickly surveyed the menu.

"What do you recommend?" said the man from out of state.

"The eight course tasting menu. Excellent," replied the local man. Both lawyers wore well tailored dark suits and silk ties.

The one from Frankfurt, Karl Schubach, looked at the eight courses and was barely impressed by the dinner prices. "OK," he said.

"Red or White?" Randolph Sutter asked.

"Red."

"Fine by me," he said as he looked down the wine list. "Pomerol. *Latour à Pomerol.*

"Yeah, I know it," Schubach said.

After the expressionless waiter had brought and poured the wine, Sutter raised his wineglass and Schubach did the same. They clicked their glasses and Sutter said, "Down the hatch. I think we need to celebrate."

"Yes," Karl Schubach replied. "This company is going to get the same as the last one."

Sutter laughed. "It's getting easier, isn't it?"

Schubach agreed. "Yeah, but we need to be careful with this one.

"It's just a matter of time."

They clicked their glasses again and each took a long drink.

During their meal, the lawyers finished a second bottle of the Pomerol. With dessert—a bittersweet chocolate tart with Calvados caramel apple sauté and vanilla bean ice cream—they ordered a bottle of the sweet Sauterne, *Chateau de Malle.*

"Brandy and cigar?" Randolph Sutter asked, as they finished.

"Of course," came the genial reply.

With these soon in hand, Karl Schubach took a sip from his brandy followed by a slow drag on the cigar. "You know, when this thing materializes we'll be set for life. But there's still the old chairman."

Randolph Sutter laughed. "Cheers. Don't worry. He won't know what hit him."

CHAPTER 12

The Café des Pescadores was one of Justin's favorites in Port de la Selva. He often bought several newspapers and had breakfast there after a run. It saved him from preparing his own food—the Señora wasn't far wrong in her assumption that he couldn't cook.

The café's sliding glass panels opened to the veranda where umbrella-topped tables shaded the packed clientele. Spanish love songs blasted out of a radio over the bar.

Justin waved to the young Señora who ran the café. She was settled in her corner on a wicker rocker, holding her six-month-old son. She smiled and pointed to a table near the window with one empty chair. Waiters flew through the crowd in a flurry of demand. After two failed attempts to catch their attention, Justin sat down to read and wait. Some minutes later, one of the waiters brought him a *café con leche*. He looked up and called "*gracias*" to the young Señora who had looked out for *El Americano*.

As he was checking to see whether his latest stocks had shifted up or down, he felt a hand on his shoulder and looked up. The waiter put down a plate of pastry in front of him and said, "*Señor Justin, telefono.*"

Justin looked to the Señora and she nodded, holding the telephone out toward him. He rose and wound around the tables to the counter, wondering who could possibly be calling him and why.

"*Gracias,*" he said as he took the telephone.

He put his hand over one ear and the telephone to the other. "This is Justin Collins."

A woman said, "Mr. Collins, could you hold a minute? Mr. Graves would like to speak with you."

A few seconds later he heard a familiar, formal British accent. "Hello, Justin. This is Charles Graves."

"Charles? This is a surprise."

"And I am surprised to have found you. My secretary called every bar, restaurant and hotel in your part of the Costa Brava. We're quite happy that she speaks Spanish, otherwise we would have been undone."

"Well, it's good to hear from you, but why all the trouble of hunting me down?"

"Justin, to be perfectly straightforward, I need your help," Charles said.

"My help?"

"Yes. We've fallen into a bit of a predicament. We need a reputable person to do an audit for us. Would you be willing to do some work in Amsterdam?"

Justin did not answer for a few seconds. On the docks beyond the umbrellas, a young boy in red shorts stood throwing bread to several seagulls. They dove for the crumbs, fighting each other with wings outspread.

Justin finally answered, "Well, I'd like to help you, but I'm currently working for a bird conservation society, tracking an endangered species of seagulls. It's pretty intensive research."

"Justin, my good man, I can offer a replacement to count the birds while you go to Amsterdam on our behalf."

"I can't," Justin turned away from the boy on the dock and continued, "I'm happy with my bird job. Don't you have plenty of auditors and financial experts in your company? Why do you need me?"

"All of our regular people are fully occupied. It has been a critical time for us, all of these scandals in the market. We received an exceptional contract from a large American company, and we want to keep it, but we must complete our audit quickly. We did subcontract pieces of it to some independent auditors, however," Charles cleared his throat, "that turned out badly."

"What went wrong?" Justin asked, curious.

"We hired an independent and sent him to Amsterdam. He had always done good work for us in the past, even though he had a reputation for being a somewhat difficult character. He spent three or four days on our job, and then he simply disappeared. We don't know where he went. Friday afternoon we made a decision to replace him. That's when I thought of you. We've been trying to find you all weekend."

"Charles, you know I'm not an accountant. My skills are in management."

"I'm speaking as your friend now, Justin," Charles said, his tone serious. "I have been thinking of you, withering away in Spain for more than half a year. I can only imagine how you've grieved, but I'm concerned that you should have the opportunity to move about in the world again. You are a talented man. I believe it's time for us to see that talent once again. Of course, I could find someone else to do the work. But you should be putting your abilities to good use."

Justin smiled. "Charles, you know if anyone else had called me, I probably would have hung up the phone. Actually it's odd—I have been thinking about starting over, but I'm not anxious to go full time. What are the parameters?"

"Right, then." Charles began, "It's simple. By the end of next week I need to have a report for the Chairman of the Board of the Unipac Corporation. He needs to help the board make a critical decision about a merger with another company, one with which you have some familiarity. We have a few of our best men auditing several sites, and we need you to carry out a short audit at one of them. This is, of course, all confidential."

"What's this about my familiarity with the other company?" Justin suddenly felt ill at ease.

"You know Unipac bought the U.S. divisions of Vine Industries, and EuroVinco acquired several of their European operations. The two companies are considering some form of partnership or a friendly merger."

"Is this your way of getting me out of the past?" Justin felt an anger rising.

"Perhaps it is a way of redeeming the past. If these two companies do merge, much of Vine Industries will have been reunited. And Sam Oliver, Unipac's Chairman, was a good friend of Peter's. Once you see his hand at the helm, you may even be pleased with yourself as having done a good deed in Peter's memory."

Justin took a deep breath. "EuroVinco was not exactly friendly when they purchased pieces of Vine."

"Unipac is aware of this. On the whole, EuroVinco is a very conservative institution. These spot audits at several EuroVinco sites help verify EuroVinco's normal auditors," Charles replied. Then he added, "Attempting to profit from a failing company is not entirely an anomaly in the business world."

"I take your point, Charles," Justin said. "But a man can learn a lot from watching birds."

"Well, if you do grow tired of doing so, you're invited to audit a small operation in Amsterdam called EuroVinco Trading."

"I promise to think about it."

Charles took this as a yes. "That's wonderful. Your flight for Amsterdam is scheduled for this evening."

"This evening?" Justin thought he'd heard wrong; the music had escalated to a thumping rhythm. "What do you mean 'this evening'?"

"Your first class tickets are already reserved. The plane leaves at 6:45 p.m. It's now 10:30 a.m. You have a good deal of time in which to reach Barcelona and board it." Charles laughed. "Enjoy your flight. Have a gin and tonic, complements of Stewart-Graves."

CHAPTER 13

Justin felt like he was wearing a foreign costume. Odd, the uniform of suit and tie had been such a part of his life for years. But for the last six months, his most formal ensemble had been a polo shirt tucked into cargo pants.

His suitcase was filled with more of the same business-like attire. He checked his watch. Almost time for Gloria's lunch break.

He pushed open the doors of the bank where she worked and crossed to her desk. "Listen Gloria, I need to go away for a couple of days on business. Would you like to have something to eat?"

"Of course," she answered, taking in the suit. She blinked. "I am surprised."

He looked down at himself. "Oh, the suit?"

"Well, we are not used to seeing you dressed up." The other employees had been staring at him. "But also this going away so suddenly."

He smiled. "Don't worry, it's just for a few days. Then I will go back to my shorts and T-shirt."

"Oh no," she shook her head, standing up, "You look very handsome like this."

They left the bank and walked to a local restaurant. Over a light lunch he told her about the phone call from Charles Graves.

Gloria waited until he finished then said, "You know, it's possible that this may be good for you. But how do you feel about going back into the business world?"

"I'm not sure, but I think I need to find out. Spending my entire life jogging along the sea may not be my calling." He gave a half-grin. "If not the business world, then I need to find something that's productive, or somewhere I can contribute."

Gloria twisted her napkin and looked up at him. "I don't mean to pry, but won't you need to make a living?"

They had never really discussed Justin's financial affairs, and the topic made him slightly uncomfortable. But Gloria was a banker—well, at least a junior banker—with all the capabilities to become a top banker some day.

"I have some money in a bank," he replied.

She waited for him to elaborate.

Justin looked out the window of the restaurant and saw a bank across the village square. It was small. A large sign in red and yellow announced it as the Banco de Balboa. How different from his bank.

He remembered the first time he entered it, in Geneva. Stefan Von Portzer had recommended it. From the outside, the bank was merely a solid looking building that resembled many others in the middle of Geneva. And like many of the old private banks, no sign marked it for what it was other than a small brass plaque outside the door. Anonymity was the goal, and over eight hundred employees worked behind those non-descript walls at keeping that goal. Justin had been ushered into a private meeting room where he had been seated in a Louis-the-Sixteenth style chair. After meeting for an hour with a knowledgeable banker, Justin had opened an account. His fortune was now being well managed by a team of highly professional people.

He repeated himself, "In a bank."

She raised an eyebrow at him, and he finally said, "Gloria, I guess you gathered that I am rather, ah, what you might say, independent. At this point finances are not one of my worries. I'm not filthy rich, but I have enough. When I left Vine Industries I had quite a few shares in the company. That plus stock options and a severance package—it adds up to an adequate amount." He paused. "And...there was the life insurance policy of Chantal and Sophie." A one-and-a-half-million-dollar policy. In the beginning it had felt like dirty money.

Gloria broke his reverie, saying, "I am glad for you that you have this. As for your future...do something that will make you happy."

He looked at her. "When I told you I loved you last night, I meant it."

Two jade eyes sparkled back. "I feel the same."

He pushed away his plate. "Well, it looks like this is getting serious."

"Yes," she said, holding the word awhile in her mouth, "but this is new to me and I need time to think about it."

He reached across and laid a finger along her cheekbone. "Well, I am gone until the end of the week. Can we talk then?"

"How about in Barcelona?" she said, brightening.

"What do you mean?" he asked.

"I am going home on Friday, to see my parents for the weekend. They told me that they would like to meet you if you ever came to Barcelona. If you are stopping there on your way back from

Amsterdam, why don't you come for lunch on Saturday or Sunday, whenever you are finished."

"That may be perfect. Depending on the audit, I should be done by the end of the week. I'll call and let you know for sure. I would enjoy seeing your parents again." He had been with her twice before to Barcelona where he had met her parents. They had warmly welcomed him. He cleared his throat. "Mostly I look forward to being with you."

"We go well together, don't we?" she asked. But it did not sound like a question.

★ ★ ★

At 5:00 A.M in San Jose, California two men got into a slate-colored Ford Expedition and started driving along Highway 17, headed towards Santa Cruz.

In half and hour, they left the highway, following a narrow winding road for several miles. They turned off onto a small dirt road that led deep into the redwood forest. About a mile up the path, they parked in a small clearing and turned off the headlights.

They unloaded two bags from the back of the Expedition and carried them off the trail, hiding them in foliage. Their observation point needed to be ready by seven o'clock.

They had been tracking their target for a week, learning his movements. Every morning at 7:00 a.m. he walked through the forest with his wife and Labrador. The dog was a concern, but if they were discovered, it would be easy for them to pass as engineers doing a survey of the forest. Their listening and recording equipment could pass as surveying instrumentation. The last two days the dog had not noticed them.

Ascertain what this man knows, they had been instructed.

Yesterday they had recorded about a third of their target's conversation during a walk with his wife. Today they hoped to do better. Best would be to identify key phrases that signaled his intentions. With better positioning, they could eventually record every word.

Their next task was to gain access to the target's house, to bug the telephone and all the rooms. A private detective had already installed listening devices in his car and his office in San Jose.

Apparently the man's son-in-law was also a target. He was some hotshot executive in a Silicon Valley company.

CHAPTER 14

A t seven p.m. Central European Time, an Iberian Airlines flight lifted off the ground, banked to the left and in a few moments was flying over the Mediterranean Sea.

Justin was not thrilled at being in a plane again. After years of business travel, he had decided that his idea of hell would entail being eternally belted into an airplane seat.

But first class—well, it helped.

The airplane was soon headed north along the Costa Brava coastline. Justin looked down at the dark blue sea below him. In the distance he could see the city of Barcelona he had just left. It was vibrant and industrious, this Catalonian capital crammed between the mountains and the sea.

The plane continued north, passing small villages along the coast and backtracking along the route he had taken by taxi from Llanca to the airport. Finally down below he saw Llanca, tiny and unimpressive from this height.

He wondered what Gloria was doing at this moment. He could still feel the soft skin of her cheek, and he held up his hand as if he would find her face there.

No Gloria. Only the stewardess bending over with a selection of juices and drinks. Why was he on this airplane?

Charles. To think that Charles had found him in an obscure little café in a small village on the Costa Brava.

Other than Charles Graves, his banker in Geneva and Stefan Von Portzer, Justin could think of no one from his business life who really knew where he was. He had known so many people in Vine Industries, yet he quickly had become an unknown. Of course, he had not tried to contact anyone.

Justin watched the coastline move below the aircraft and soon the water disappeared and they were over land again, flying over Southern France. He opened his copy of the Herald Tribune. He turned first to the listing of the New York stock exchange, but he realized it was Monday and the Friday stock markets had already been listed in the weekend edition.

He started to turn to the sports page, but a short article caught his interest on the first page of the business section. It read:

Until now, the merger discussions had been conducted in secret. Charles had told him that the name of Unipac was to be kept confidential, but rumors were starting to hit the street. No wonder Charles wanted to move so quickly on this audit.

At the same time, he wondered why there was a $125 M loss for the quarter with such good sales growth. And, on the growth side, was it real business growth, or just the result of adding the European pieces of Vine Industries into EuroVinco's financial statements? In any case, this little audit in Amsterdam was a mere technicality as far as the merger went.

The plane passed over Belgium and began its descent into Amsterdam's Schipol Airport. Justin began to feel apprehensive. Before he started his Masters Degree, he had worked a year and a half for an accounting firm in Los Angeles in order to pay off his school loans. The accounting company provided auditing services to its clients, and Justin had participated in several of these audits. He understood the processes one followed, but that was some time ago. He feared his skills might be rusty.

He told himself that inspecting a subsidiary business unit like EuroVinco Trading was straightforward—especially if another auditor had already done most of the job.

How strange that the auditor had just disappeared. It seemed out of character for Charles Graves to hire an unreliable person—unless something else happened to the man.

He looked through the window and saw the port of Rotterdam to his left. He glanced at the peaceful lights below and reassured himself that there was no great pressure in doing this assignment, other than to verify a few company records. A change is as good as a rest, so they said in England.

Justin sighed, thinking that in just three uneventful days in Amsterdam he could get back to his quiet life and love in Spain.

* * *

As Justin's plane descended into Amsterdam, a telephone rang in the South of France. After two rings, someone answered it.

"Who is it?"

"West Coast." The man in California did not like to use his name. He was a surveillance man.

"This is Spiros, go ahead."

"Just to let you know we had a good fix on the target."

"How much did you get?" Spiros asked.

"About half their conversation."

"That's doing better. Where does he stand?"

"From what we can tell, he's cautious, but perhaps he's moving closer to the concept."

"Good. *Le Patron* called a few minutes ago and is anxious to know what's going on. He wants to know when we will receive the recording."

The mention of *Le Patron* caused the West Coast man to come to attention. There were rumors about *Le Patron*. Some people said he did not exist, that he was a fictitious figure used by the French organization. Other rumors said he was ruthless. Still, West Coast knew he was being well paid for his work. Whether *Le Patron* was real or not, significant amounts had been deposited in his bank account, and an even greater amount was waiting for him when his job was completed.

"The recording is currently being prepared and will be transmitted to you in the next two hours," West Coast replied.

Spiros needed to get his two computer engineers back into the office to work on the data. They had gone home already. It was going to be a late night for them.

"OK, we will be expecting the transmission in two hours," Spiros said. " Keep up your surveillance. Did you get a listening device in his home yet?"

"No not yet. There are people there most of the time and they have a dog. We need to be careful."

"Well, just get it done as soon as possible. And bug his wife's car. I want to know every single word that comes out of his mouth."

The line went dead before West Coast could respond.

CHAPTER 15

Amsterdam, The Netherlands

The EuroVinco Trading receptionist greeted Justin with a smile. "Good morning. How may I help you?"

"My name is Justin Collins, from Stewart-Graves. I have an appointment with Mr. Maertens."

When she heard the name Stewart-Graves the receptionist looked down at the papers in front of her, remembering the horrid Mr. McDowell who had been here the week before. The man standing before her was entirely different—tall, tan and handsome. And those eyes. She looked back at him

"Yes, I will call him immediately. He is expecting you."

In a few minutes, a middle-aged man in a dark blue business suit walked into the room. Justin was reminded of a used-car salesman.

"Hello Mr. Collins, my name is Jan Maertens, Managing Director of EuroVinco Trading." He flashed a smile. "Mr. Graves called me yesterday afternoon and said you would arrive this morning. We are anxious to have the audit done and will do anything possible to help you in any way."

"Thank you and it's a pleasure to meet you," Justin said, knowing the man was buttering sincerity over a slice of artificiality. No company enjoyed having an audit.

Jan Maertens flashed a large smile. "Could you please come with me?"

★ ★ ★

"I hope you don't mind if we put you up here. As you saw, we are very full downstairs."

"Why is this area empty?" Justin asked. He and Maertens had taken the stairs up to the second floor and were standing in a large, vacant office space. Three smaller, windowed offices lined the back.

"This is where the Specialized Trading Department used to be."

"What was that?"

"That's a bit of a mystery. Until last week there were five or six people working up here and sometimes seven or eight. The people in my organization downstairs were jealous because things are so crowded down there. Look around. You could put over twenty people in this room, but someone in top management wanted it that way. I tried to fight it through with my manager at the EuroVinco headquarters in London, but there seemed to be political battles in upper management and I didn't win."

"What did the Specialized Trading Department do?" Justin tried again.

"Well, to be honest, we didn't know much about them. All I know is that they were handling the trading of products, and they were known to be providing back-office work for some other parts of the EuroVinco Corporation."

"What products did they deal in?"

"Honestly, Mr. Collins, I have no idea. They didn't report to me. They were a special unit reporting to an office in Nice, France. That office sent them directives and also did some trading with them, I think. We were instructed to stay out of it. They even had their own entrance. The stairs we just climbed were never used, and the metal door was locked much of the time."

Justin looked around the room. It was empty, except for some pictures and a calendar on the wall. In one of the offices, papers lay scattered around a pile of boxes in a corner.

"When did they move out?"

"Over the weekend. Shortly after the, er, last auditor left." Martens made a look of distaste.

"What happened to their desks and chairs and files?"

"On Saturday the movers came in and cleared most of it out, except for the few things in the corner, which they said they will remove so that we can refurnish the place. I guess everything was moved back to Nice. I can now move my people up here." Maertens was obviously pleased about the turn of events and equally disinterested in the vanished workers who had made it possible.

Justin decided not to pursue it. He set down his briefcase and turned to Maertens, "Why don't we get started with the audit?"

⋆ ⋆ ⋆

Justin sat at a desk with the small piles of papers Mr. McDowell had left behind. The office smelled of stale cigarette smoke.

He looked out through the glass window into the large empty room, drumming his fingers. The only thing he had wanted in the past six months was solitude, and now that he was back in the work world, he felt uncomfortably alone.

He pulled out the audit checklist Charles had sent to the Apollo Hotel where he was staying.

It was Tuesday morning. If things went smoothly, he would be on the Thursday evening flight back to Barcelona. Motivation enough.

He shuffled through McDowell's papers, noting the precise handwriting. It was odd to be going through the papers of a man who just disappeared. Coffee stains and cigarette smoke spotted some of the scrap papers. The man had been orderly with numbers but not with much else.

Over the following hours Justin slowly verified the accuracy of McDowell's records and built a clear report of the company's profit and loss statements. He worked until eight in the evening, ordered a taxi and waited outside the office for about five minutes, enjoying the cool air of the evening.

The street was dark and empty, except for a man sitting alone on a brick step across the street. Justin had a fleeting impression that the man was looking at him—his eyes darted erratically from Justin to the street and back. Justin was glad when the taxi came.

⋆ ⋆ ⋆

The following morning, Justin returned to the upstairs office space. Instead of going into the room he was using, he found himself poking around the office next to his where the stack of cardboard boxes held the last remnants of the peculiar Specialized Trading Department.

Get on with business, he told himself, and went back to his desk.

He worked hard through the day, going through papers, double-checking McDowell's material and adding to it. He did not enjoy this type of work and was glad he had chosen another career path.

This would be a one-time event, Justin decided, unless Charles twisted his arm again. If he went back to full-time work, things would be different.

Well, at least everything seemed to be in order so far. If the remaining records proved clean and exact, his report to Charles Graves would be favorable—and completed soon.

He had been looking at his watch all day in anticipation of phoning Gloria. He knew she would be leaving the bank at six thirty. At six o'clock, he dialed her bank in Spain. He gave his name and asked for her. A minute later she was on the line.

He felt nervous.

"Hello," she said, affection and expectation contained in two syllables.

"Hello, Gloria." Justin's own voice was husky with wanting to say this to her face, not to a phone receiver.

And not countries away.

CHAPTER 16

Based on a review of the operations following a strict methodology, I believe that the consolidated profit and loss and other key financial statements accurately reflect the current financial position of EuroVinco Trading, and in my opinion, proper business controls were in place during the past fiscal year.

With that, Justin concluded his audit report.

It was late on Wednesday evening. For two days he had worked twelve hours at a time, his nose deep in papers.

He pushed back from his chair, stretching his long arms up. He missed running and wanted to move. He tossed a crumpled paper in the wastebasket and stood up, looking around him as if for inspiration.

He walked into the room where the "remains" of the curious Specialized Trading Department were stacked in cardboard boxes. He read over the white shipping labels that read "Marché Transport" with an address in Villepinte, France.

Justin knew Villepinte, having lived in Paris for six years. It lay a few kilometers south of Charles de Gaulle airport and spanned a large industrial zone of shipping companies, offices, and small manufacturing operations.

Lifting and shifting the boxes, Justin noticed that the shipping labels were all the same, but that someone had also hand-written the names of different companies on the boxes. Some of the names he recognized.

At the bottom of the stack he saw "Vine Industries."

Vine Industries had used the services of EuroVinco Trading a number of times in the past, but that was five years ago and the dates on this information were recent. Justin pulled the small box out from the pile and removed the tape. Flipping through, he found a file for Vine at the bottom and took it back into his small office.

Puzzling—here were records of electronic equipment shipped to Middle Eastern countries. This was something they had not done before. The file also held documents in French, Arabic and other languages he did not even recognize.

Justin spent thirty minutes going through the maze of files, trying to decode them. At least they were in chronological order. He worked his way through a year of data until he eventually came across some papers dated from the previous August.

Three papers stapled together caught his attention. The first was an order from a factory in Romania by the name of Locomotiva Bucheristi. The second was the shipment record of the goods being transported to France. The company making the shipment was Marché Transport.

On the third page he saw a hand-written record confirming that the goods were loaded on an airplane. The plane's registration numbers were A776-507. The date was August fourteenth, almost one year ago.

Justin's head began to spin.

* * *

In the Redwood forest near their Santa Cruz ranch, Sam and Margaret Oliver watched their Labrador emerge from the brush with a stick in his mouth and drop it at Sam's feet. The dog turned, cocked his head to one side, and started barking.

Sam patted the dog on the back. "It's ok, Buck. Quiet down. You'll wake up the neighbors."

Buck restlessly repositioned his feet and stood, whining. Stiffening his tail, he set his nose to the ground, sniffing out an unmarked yet distinct path into the forest.

Once out of sight, Buck began barking again.

Sam and Margaret walked along a winding path whose loamy soil gave gently beneath their feet. They reached a clearing where the sun broke through the trees and morning mist and sat together on a log.

Buck appeared again only to rush past them in pursuit of a brown squirrel.

"That dog is a muddy mess," Margaret said as she and Sam watched Buck turn and run at full speed into a small creek.

Sam said nothing for several minutes. Finally he sighed, "We've got some big decisions."

"You mean the merger with EuroVinco? " she asked.

"Yes. This is one of the most important things we've done in Unipac," he said. At sixty-nine years old, Sam Oliver was now the Chairman of the Board of the Unipac Corporation, a Fortune 500 company.

"So, what are you thinking?" Margaret asked.

Sam paused for a moment. "As I said, this is a big decision. Big financial implications. But it could strengthen the company by providing a stronger base in Europe."

"Will you go through with it?" Margaret asked

"Well, you know me, I just need to know that all the angles have been considered."

Margaret turned toward the direction of Buck's barking but could not see him.

"What's your deadline for the decision?" she asked, turning again toward Sam.

"Unipac's Board of Directors meets next week and that's when we need to make our formal go-ahead. From that point on things would move quickly."

"And you're hesitating because?"

"I'm not sure. I guess it has to do with the fit between Unipac and EuroVinco, but also the fact that I don't really understand the European market. It's a complex environment over there. Maybe it's just a fear of the unknown."

"Maybe it has to do with values," Margaret suggested, leaning her shoulder toward his and then back.

He smiled at her. "How do you maintain a value system in another corporate culture? You know, I've said it a thousand times," Sam continued. "People are the most important thing at Unipac. Saying it and demonstrating it is the reason people in the company have trusted me. Yet I've often questioned myself on this statement. Are they important because they are productive and create profit, or are they important because they have intrinsic value in themselves, completely unrelated to the profit."

"Always the philosopher." She patted his knee and continued, "Sam, have you thought that—"

"Wait, wait a second," he interrupted, holding up his palm. "Listen. Did you hear that?"

"Hear what?"

"I thought I heard voices."

"What voices?"

"Mens' voices. Listen."

Margaret turned her ear in the direction he had pointed. "I don't hear anything."

"I could have sworn I heard something. Sorry, honey. What were you saying?"

"Have you thought that you might have to travel to Europe more?" She asked.

"I'm tired of airplanes."

"You could visit Anne," Margaret suggested, referring to their granddaughter who was doing graduate study at Cambridge University.

Sam laughed. "You mean we go and spend billions of dollars to buy a European company so that I can go and visit my granddaughter?"

"Call it icing on the cake."

"OK. That's a great reason for buying EuroVinco. Let me think how to explain that one to the shareholders."

They laughed while Buck barked in the trees.

CHAPTER 17

Amsterdam, The Netherlands

Justin leaned against the wall for support. August fourteenth—the date of the police report, of the life-insurance policy.

He closed his eyes and was back on the Parisian sidewalk with his cell phone in hand, hearing of his wife's death.

He could not explain it, but while still spinning from memory, he walked straight for the Xerox machine in the outer office and photocopied the three papers. He returned to his office and looked quickly through the rest of the chronological file but found nothing related to these three pieces of paper.

On the top sheet, the contents of the shipment read "Electronic Components." This was strange. What would Pete Vine want with components coming from Romania? Vine Industries owned entire factories that could make any electrical device you could imagine. And why would Pete have taken them on board that passenger flight?

Justin thought back to the time he had dealt with EuroVinco Trading five years before. These transactions could relate to those dealings, or then again, this could be something more recent. August fourteenth was some months before the break-up of Vine Industries. Justin had no recollection of ever having done business with a Romanian company, nor did he remember this "Specialized Trading Department." Of course, he had been operating out of the Vine Industries' European headquarters in Paris and it was impossible for him to know of every European transaction.

He put the photocopies into his briefcase and made his way downstairs to the lobby. It was past ten o'clock. The security guard, thinking the building empty, was surprised to see him. Without a word, he went to the front door and unlocked it. Justin thanked the man and left the building.

The night was cool and the fresh air revived him. He had spent the whole day sitting inside and needed to walk.

Justin followed one of the canals, absorbed in his discovery. The street was empty except for three men some hundred meters behind him. He looked back and they stopped and started to talk, but it made him feel uneasy. He decided that the papers he had found had unsettled him, but he continued to watch the men. At one point they separated and he decided that they were not a threat.

At length, he walked toward a main street and signaled a free taxi to the Apollo Hotel.

★ ★ ★

Justin slept fitfully, but somehow he was out cold when the telephone rang. He reached over and knocked the receiver on the floor, picked it up and rasped, "Hello."

"This is your wakeup call," a real voice informed him.

Half asleep, he moaned "Thank you," and missed the cradle when he tried to set it down. The receiver dropped to the floor again with a thud that brought the business and personal nature of August fourteenth back to him.

He cut his face while shaving, skipped breakfast, and ten minutes later checked out of the hotel. In the taxi ride to the office, he looked in the rearview mirror and saw that his jaw was still bleeding. He swore and pressed a handkerchief to the cut.

He was going to look at every paper in those boxes.

At quarter to eight, he was standing in the room where yesterday he had found the box marked "Vine Industries."

Everything was gone.

Had he imagined those pages? To reassure himself, he opened his briefcase and found the photocopies. *Right then*, he thought, *not crazy*. But definitely on to something fishy.

He went back downstairs and entered Maertens' office, forgetting to knock. "Mr. Maertens. What happened to the cardboard boxes that were in the office upstairs?"

Jan Maertens looked up. "I am sorry—what boxes?"

"Come with me," Justin told him.

Both men proceeded to the upper floor. Justin pointed to the empty office and said, "Over there. Where are the boxes that were in the room over there?"

"Oh yes, I do remember boxes," Maertens said, as if remembering that he had toast for breakfast.

"They were there last night at ten, and now they are not here at eight the following morning. I think you'd agree that we aren't dealing with elves or fairies. Who took them? I need to look into those boxes."

Maertens held up placating hands. "Don't worry, Mr. Collins. I will find out what happened."

Maertens turned and disappeared down the stairs, returning in a bit of a pant ten minutes later. "I had to call the security guard and wake him up from his sleep. He was not very happy, but he did tell me that last night the shipping company came by to pick up the missing boxes."

"Which shipping company?"

"We don't know. We think it was the French one whose name was on the boxes, but no one knows for sure. They were probably the ones who came on Saturday and took all the desks and chairs and files. By the way, I tried to call Mr. Schneider in Nice yesterday to get more information about the Specialized Trading Department."

"Who is Mr. Schneider?"

"He works within the EuroVinco Corporation but is located in Nice. Mr. Schneider was the liaison from EuroVinco to the Specialized Trading Department. I wasn't sure if the supervisor here, Mr. Ziginiglou, reported to him or not."

"Mr. Ziginiglou? Can you spell that for me?" Justin asked.

Maertens did and continued, "He was the supervisor of the Specialized Trading Department. He was an accountant—Greek, I think. He was a difficult man to talk with, but he ran a very tight department. I can't tell you much more than that."

"So, what did this Mr. Schneider say?"

"I tried to call him, but he wasn't there. When I called Nice they told me that Mr. Schneider is not working there anymore."

Justin picked up his briefcase and extended a hand. "Thank you for your help, Mr. Maertens." He was almost to the stairs when he turned around and added, "By the way, you passed the audit fine. EuroVinco Trading is in good health."

CHAPTER 18

It looked like his itinerary was going to change. He had to locate this Marché Transport, and it was based in Villepinte—conveniently near the airport. But inconveniently near Paris. Paris was the last place Justin wanted to go.

He waved down a taxi and with as little enthusiasm as he could, said, "Schipol airport, please." They pulled away and into traffic, neither

Justin nor the driver noticing a certain sedan following behind them.

At the airport, Justin headed to the KLM desk to change his ticket and arranged to get on the next flight to Paris.

Once through customs, he made his way to a post office offering fax services and handed his audit to the young man behind the counter, asking that it be faxed to Stewart-Graves in London. Once the fax was completed, Justin placed the report into an Express mailer and asked, "How long will it take to get to London?"

"It should be there this afternoon, but definitely by tomorrow."

Justin thanked the man and asked if he could make a call. He was directed to one of the empty booths along the wall.

He dialed London.

The Stewart-Graves operator transferred him through to Charles.

"Hello Charles, this is Justin."

"Justin! How are you doing? Are you calling from Amsterdam?"

"Yes, I'm at the airport. The audit is finished. The report was faxed to you a few minutes ago. Did you receive it?" Justin decided not to mention the photocopies he held in his briefcase.

"It's being placed on my desk as we speak."

"I'm also sending you a hard copy by Express mail, and you should receive it today or tomorrow."

"How did it go?" Charles asked.

"I made it through every boring item on your list," he laughed. "To be honest, when you called me in Spain I never thought I could do this."

"So, it was a good step back into the real world?"

"It was easier than I imagined. In fact, most of the hard work had already been done by Mr. McDowell. It would have taken me twice as much time without his material."

"Yes, we feel terrible about his disappearance last Thursday night. In spite of his idiosyncrasies, he was an excellent auditor." Charles sounded regretful.

"Last Thursday night, you said?"

"Yes. He was at EuroVinco Trading on Thursday, but it appears he wasn't at the hotel on Thursday night. All his personal things were there on Friday morning and the bed had not been slept in. As I said, he just disappeared."

"What a shame," Justin said casually, thinking about the audit reports from Dick McDowell. This meant that he only had the man's papers from Monday to Wednesday. If McDowell had been working on Thursday, then what happened to the audit records for that day?

"Well Justin, tell me what you found," Charles said.

"Nothing. Well, almost nothing. Overall the business is in good order. The cash position is correct, receivables are what they should be, and the balance sheet works out. It's all in the report."

"Good news, Justin, good news. I'm catching a flight to San Francisco this afternoon where I have a meeting with Unipac's CFO. It seems that our report to the Board of Directors will be positive."

"Charles, I believe I'm going to buy myself a billion shares of Unipac," Justin said, biting the inside of his cheek to keep from laughing.

As Justin had hoped, Charles' voice rose above his usual monotone. "Don't you dare! Insider trading wouldn't go over well with the U.S. Securities and Exchange Commission." He continued in humorous relief, "Seriously, you know that this must be considered confidential. Rumors are already out on the street and the share prices of Unipac and EuroVinco are getting jittery."

"You know I was kidding. Just wanted to see if I could shake you up a bit. But honestly, how do you think these two companies will fit together?"

Charles hesitated for a moment. "In terms of products it is a good fit. The two companies will leverage off of each other. Culturally there might be some questions, except that Unipac is considered the buyer in the exchange of shares and that puts them in the driving seat. But, they will have their hands full for a while."

"What do you mean?" Justin asked.

"Internally EuroVinco is a maze of different legal entities and structures. It's crazy, and they have three corporate headquarters, in London, Frankfurt and Nice."

"Why so many and why Nice?"

"Nice is one of the leading high-tech centers in France, along with Grenoble and Lyon, so I guess it's important for them to have an operation there."

Something occurred to Justin and he asked, "Who are the major shareholders of EuroVinco?"

"Financial institutions and holding companies, each with different structures depending on the country where they are based. The largest is a company called GauLux Holding."

"I heard something about GauLux Holding when Vine Industries was being broken up," Justin said. "Doesn't some flamboyant French businessman–politician represent GauLux Holding on the EuroVinco board of directors?"

"Yes, from what we can gather, the entire board of EuroVinco is full of flamboyant characters. As I said, Unipac will have their hands full, but don't you think Pete Vine would be pleased that Vine Industries is coming back together under Unipac?"

"I think so." *A nice irony,* Justin thought to himself. He had helped Pete Vine build Vine Industries, at least the Vine Industries operations in Europe, and now he was making a recommendation on the future of the company.

Justin decided to ask, "Hey, by the way, did you ever hear of a 'Specialized Trading Department' in EuroVinco Amsterdam?"

There was a pause and Charles answered, "No. I have never heard of it. Why do you ask?"

"Well, it appears there was a unique department that was part of EuroVinco and was based in the same building in Amsterdam as EuroVinco Trading. It's not there anymore, but I just wondered if it showed up anywhere in the overall legal structure of EuroVinco."

"No, I never saw it," Charles replied. "Did we miss something?"

"Well, it's no longer there, so I guess there is nothing to miss. I'm just wondering—was the Specialized Trading Department listed as being one of the operations to be audited in EuroVinco?"

Justin heard scuffling of papers. "Justin, I have a list of all the EuroVinco subsidiaries. That one is not on the list. Are you sure we didn't miss something?"

"Perhaps. I don't know." Justin paused and thought about that question and wasn't sure what to tell Charles so he said, "Probably not. I really can't say. It was just a question."

"Justin, before I forget, how can I get in touch with you? We had to make a lot of telephone calls last weekend."

"I've asked the Spanish telephone company to install a phone in my place, but it is taking time. For the moment, it's best to leave a message for me at Eusebi's in Llanca—a barbershop. It's better than trying to track me through all the bars and restaurants in the Costa Brava." Justin cleared his throat and said, "And by the way, thanks for this opportunity."

"I am the one that should be saying thanks. What do you plan next?"

"I'm headed back to Spain. How can I put it?"

He closed his eyes. "There is a beautiful young woman down there who is waiting for me."

CHAPTER 19

A telephone rang in the South of France and after two rings a voice answered, "Who is it?"

"Ziginiglou."

"Hello Ziginiglou, this is Spiros. *Le Patron* wants to talk with you. Hold on."

Ziginiglou did not like this. Speaking to Spiros was one thing. Spiros was a coordinator operating under the commands of *Le Patron*. Most of Ziginiglou's day-to-day contact was with Spiros. Speaking directly to *Le Patron* sent shivers down his spine. Ziginiglou had met the man five times and had disliked each occasion.

He had heard stories. *Le Patron* was tribal, a tyrant chieftain demanding absolute loyalty and obedience. There were consequences for falling short, and once you were part of the tribe there was no way out.

Ziginiglou tried to remember the rules for speaking with *Le Patron* on the phone: only short phrases, no names of people, places, or companies, unless he asked for specific information.

He waited, not sure if *Le Patron* was on the line. "Hello?" Ziginiglou spoke.

"What is the status?" The voice was cold and hard.

"We believe it acceptable review," replied Ziginiglou.

"Explain."

"The reviewer finished his work today. It is assumed clean."

"I don't like the word assumed."

Ziginiglou realized he had chosen the wrong word. English was not his native tongue. "I mean no evidence shows that cleanup action is necessary."

"There better not be. Two auditors disappearing within two weeks. This would cause suspicion," *Le Patron* answered. Ziginiglou could not tell whether this had been sarcastic or not.

"All evidence is removed on weekend. We completed the moving job Sunday, and the office was empty Monday. There was nothing for the reviewer to find."

"Where are your employees and the records?"

Ziginiglou swallowed hard and answered, "The employees are moved to temporary location, a guesthouse in Paris. They are five, and they are under control. They know nothing of sensitivity of operation.

They are just accountants. The records—they being destroyed."

There was a moment of silence, and then *Le Patron* said, "I want you to move your accountants to the office in the South of France.

Being summoned to the South of France meant Ziginiglou would be involved in the core operations and the remuneration would be considerably larger. And so would the consequences for unacceptable work.

Ziginiglou tried to focus—*Le Patron* was asking for an update.

"Last weekend, after the first one had accident in canal, the place was wipe clean as we agreed. The new auditor came for three days, actually two, and couple of hours this morning. He has been under surveillance since arrival. Your three helpers have been follow him always, except for time he in the office. He did nothing special and worked long days. Only go between office to the hotel. Today at noon they followed him to the airport."

"What was his destination?"

"We do not know."

The line was quiet for a moment. "What do you mean, you don't know?"

"All we know is, he sent by the audit company, the financial services company from London. We think he came from London. Probably went back to London."

"I also don't like the word 'probably'," *Le Patron* said. "But the important thing is what is in his report. I need to know exactly what is going to be sent by the financial services company to the target corporation in the U.S. We need advance information in case we need to become more proactive."

Ziginiglou remained quiet. He didn't want to tell *Le Patron* that the three men had gotten blocked in traffic following Collins to the airport. By the time they got to Schipol airport they had lost him. The target had already gone through customs.

"Ziginiglou, I want you to get some air tickets for our three friends. They should visit the office in London to obtain a copy of the final report that will go to the target in America. Do you understand?"

Ziginiglou realized that his name had been used. He swallowed. "Sir, as you instruct, they will go to London on next airplane and get information quick."

"Good. We need to stay on top of this thing. Tell me, what do you know about the auditor? Was he a direct employee of the financial company in London, or was he an independent contractor like the last one?"

"We are not sure about that. We moved out of office on the weekend. I could not go back to find information on him. All I know is that our informant found his name."

"What is it?"

"Do you want me to say name over telephone?"

"Ye-e-s," *Le Patron's* voice was definitely sarcastic this time.

"Justin Collins."

A few seconds later, Ziginiglou heard laughter. It sounded like a laugh of denial. No, it was an evil laugh. Ziginiglou waited for it to stop and then asked, "Do you know this man?"

The voice laughed again and said, "You might say this is unexpected. I understand why the financial services company would call on him with his knowledge of the parties involved. What a surprise. I thought this man was out of the picture."

Ziginiglou did not understand, but asked, "We do something special?"

"Yes. Be very careful. Track him down, but stay out of sight. Six months ago he disappeared, which was an acceptable solution for me. Now he reappears. It may be better if he disappeared again, permanently, and we may have to arrange that. Do not take any action without checking with me. I want Spiros to manage any cleanup operation. This auditor is insignificant. If he disappears quietly on his own, that is sufficient for me. When our three friends visit the financial services company, they should also try to find out where this auditor lives."

"I will instruct as according your wishes," replied Ziginiglou.

"If our three friends are able to find Collins's location, I want them to keep an eye on him, to track him to see if he does anything unusual. We will keep surveillance in place until our main objective has been achieved."

"It may be difficult to know where he is. He left here three hours before and I think he goes to London, but we will do our best."

"All I can say is that you better do two things if you want a job in the South of France. First, get a copy of the report that is going to the U.S. Second, get Collins's address. Do you understand?"

"Yes sir." Ziginiglou understood. He understood that this meant promotion or his end.

The cold voice again said, "Do you understand?"

"Yes sir," Ziginiglou responded again.

"Keep me informed."

The line clicked dead. Ziginiglou let out a long breath. Not even setting down the receiver, he immediately placed another call.

He needed the three men to take action now.

CHAPTER 20

Paris

Justin sighed.

At least he did not have to go into the city. He entered the Charles de Gaulle Airport terminal. He could navigate through the place with his eyes closed—all those years of leaving and returning on business. He wished he could keep his eyes closed and not look, not remember when this was home.

At the car-rental agency, he had a choice between a red Renault and a blue Peugeot. He left the maze of terminal roads in the red car. The Peugeot was the same model Chantal had driven.

He found the autoroute and in a few minutes he was in Villepinte. After some searching, he located the address he was looking for. A large five-story building, it housed at least thirty companies according to the sign near its entrance. Marché Transport was not one of them.

Justin rang for the concierge. After a few minutes a small man with balding hair and thick spectacles came to the door.

"*Bonjour monsieur,*" Justin said.

The man greeted Justin gruffly. A televised soccer game was on at full volume in the next room. The man craned his neck backward to watch a player in blue try for the goal.

When he had turned back, Justin continued in French, "*Monsieur,* I'm looking for a company called Marché Transport at this address. Can you tell me which floor they occupy?"

"*Ils sont plus là.*"

"Not here anymore? Have they moved?" Justin asked, surprised.

"As I said, they are not here anymore. They paid rent for a two-year contract, but vacated this past weekend. Their office is empty and it's still paid-up for another six months. It was a very strange company. It's full of *pieds-noirs*. These kind of people should not be doing business in France anyway." Justin had heard this derogatory term before. It literally meant 'black feet' and referred to North African immigrants. He decided to ignore the slur.

"Do you have any idea at all what happened to them? I would appreciate any information you can give me."

"*Attendez un moment monsieur.* I will look to see what I can find." The concierge disappeared into his office, pausing to check on the game. Five minutes later, he brought Justin a hand written address: "Louis Abdouelle, 25 rue Augustine in Paris."

Justin went back to the car and took out a map of Paris. He had an idea of the 'arrondissement,' or neighborhood where he could find 'Rue Augustine,' but it was a small street. After some searching, he found it near the Gare de Lyon. He was unfamiliar with this part of town. It had become a ghetto for many North Africans from former French colonies.

Well. It looked like he was going back into the heart of Paris after all. And at rush hour on the *Peripherique* autoroute.

* * *

Three men walked off an Amsterdam flight into London Heathrow. As they made their way through the terminal, they separated and went through customs at two-minute intervals.

Yass, the first man, wore a business suit. At customs he walked through the 'European Union Only' line, holding his French passport shoulder-high so that the customs agent could see it.

The customs agent did glance his way. The large scar running down Yass's Middle Eastern features did nothing to improve his already menacing appearance.

Yass slipped his passport in his pocket and headed toward the shuttle bus pickup area. Had the customs agent stopped him and opened his passport he would have read the name of 'Alain Naffic,' a name given to him by his French uncle. For personal reasons he preferred to go by Yass. It was closer to his original name given to him by his mother.

The three men met up, got in a rental car, and headed for London. Valentine drove. Turk rode shotgun and was the first one to speak. "Quit driving so fast." Valentine just smiled and accelerated.

"Why can't they drive on the normal side of the road like everyone else?" Turk asked of the passenger window. "The British are strange. The entire world drives normal except for the British."

"Shut up Turk," Valentine told him.

Yass sat in the back and remained quiet. He glared at the back of Valentine's nervous, twitching English head. Then he glared at the three-quarter profile of Turk, with only slightly less hatred. The only time his face relaxed its tight dislike was when they passed a mosque, its minarets glowing gold in the evening sun.

Yass and Turk had worked together for some time. Yass had met him while they were working for the Albanians, and at some point the Albanians had sent them to *Le Patron*. Turk was thick-headed, but he took orders and followed them. For Yass, Turk's biggest weakness was his lack of religious conviction.

Like Turk, Yass had been educated in a country that was not his own. But unlike Turk, Yass had not integrated into his adopted culture. His uncle, who ran a religious community in a run-down section of Marseille in the south of France, had ensured that Yass remained unpolluted. The uncle liked to call himself an *Imam*, but most Islamic communities in France did not acknowledge or have anything to do with him. He defined extremism.

Turk turned around to Yass and pleaded, "Tell him to slow down. He's crazy."

"Slow down," Yass commanded.

A moment later Valentine took his foot off the accelerator. No one in the car said a word.

Yass scratched his cheek, not even feeling the scar he had worn so long. It was as much a part of his hard face as his nose and certainly larger. His Palestinian mother had named him 'Yassar' in honor of the great freedom fighter. Yass had earned that scar in his first true fight—at age eleven. The other boy died before his wounds even had a chance to stop bleeding.

Several kilometers later, Valentine finally spoke. "Where do we go?"

"Head for the financial district," Yass answered.

"What are we supposed to do here?" asked Turk.

"Our job," said Yass.

★ ★ ★

After navigating through the small streets behind the Gare de Lyon, Justin found Rue Augustine. Couscous restaurants, bargain clothing stores, and bookshops advertised their wares in Arabic and French. Men in full-length robes of solid beige or gray stripes and women in head coverings walked past him. He felt more conscious of his suit than when he had walked into Gloria's bank.

He found a parking lot and locked his car, keeping his passport, air tickets and the three photocopied pieces of paper in his jacket pocket.

He made his way down Rue Augustine, looking for number twenty-five. Several blocks down the street he found the *'Agence Immobilière'*. Inside, a heavy-set receptionist with dyed blonde hair looked up from her *'Paris Match'* magazine.

Justin smiled. *"Bonjour madame. Je cherche Monsieur Abdouelle. Est-ce qu'il est là?"*

"Il n'est pas là. Il revient dans une demi-heure."

He had to wait half an hour.

CHAPTER 21

Louis Abdouelle was a small man with a large stomach. He was smoking a Gauloise cigarette and blowing smoke out in front of his grease-stained tie.

Justin had hoped to speak with Mr. Abdouelle in private, but his secretary lingered in the office, shuffling papers around until Abdouelle motioned with his eyes and head toward the door. She walked out of the room but left the door open. Abdouelle got up and shut it. *"Les secretaires,"* he said, flinging an arm in the direction she had gone. He sat down, gestured for Justin to do the same, and waited for him to speak.

"Mr. Abdouelle," Justin said, " I'm looking for a company called Marché Transport. The Concierge at their old office in Villepinte said that you might be able to help me find them."

"Sorry," he said, "I don't know any company called Marché Transport." He looked at the tailoring of Justin's suit. "But my memory is not too good sometimes."

Justin reached into his wallet and pulled out a fifty-euro note and held it in his hand.

Louis Abdouelle straightened in his chair. *"Ah, oui.* Let me think."

Justin put the euro note in his shirt pocket and waited.

Finally Abdouelle said, "Yes, I do remember something," He leaned slightly forward. "What do you need to know?"

"Where I can find Marché Transport. And anything else you know about them.”

“Actually I know very little about them. Over a year ago they asked me to find an office near Charles de Gaulle Airport. I found an office, rented it, and was paid by them. That is all.”

“Who was the person you dealt with in Marché Transport, and where can I find that person?”

“I don’t remember. It was such a long time ago,” Abdouelle said sincerely.

“You don’t remember anything? A name?”

“Not really,” Abdouelle said, looking annoyed.

“Then the information you give me is really worth nothing,” Justin said, starting to stand and pocketing the bill.

Abdouelle motioned with his hand to sit down. “Wait a minute. Let me look through my files.” He turned to a table behind his desk and started looking through piles of paper, folders and envelopes. A few sheets went flying onto the floor. Justin doubted this man could find anything with such a filing system. After dislodging several precarious stacks, Abdouelle retrieved an old folder with a single sheet in it. “*Ah, voila*, here it is. Now I remember.” He spun back around in his chair and continued, “It was a Mr. Khanoum and his address is 35, Rue de Lille, several streets from here. I was never there, and that is all I can tell you. I have not heard from him for over a year. The deal was transacted and that was it.”

Abdouelle stood up. “Now,” he said, looking at the pocket where Justin had stuck the bill, “regarding our arrangement?”

⋆ ⋆ ⋆

Justin asked directions from a woman sitting behind a small newspaper stand. One hundred meters beyond, he turned left toward the Rue de Lille. The small streets were closer here, and Justin felt eyes following him.

Rue de Lille looked more like a back alley. It was a dead-end street. He found the building he wanted and a row of mailboxes with green labels inside. The name Shafi Khanoum was pasted above the next-to-last mailbox with ‘3me, appt. 310’ lettered beneath.

Justin entered the stairwell through a metal door with a hole where its handle once was. He started climbing to the third floor, each wooden stair creaking under his weight. The heavy smells of spices, mildew, cigarette smoke, and hot grease hung in the thick, still air. A dim light came from above.

He reached the second floor, sensed movement, and stopped. At the end of the dark hall he thought he saw someone. He blinked slowly, letting his eyes adjust to the darkness.

Reaching the third floor, he left the stairwell and found himself in a dingy hallway lined with brown-paneled doors on either side. He proceeded forward, eyeing the number on the first door to his right: '3_7'. The middle digit was missing. He moved farther down the hall until he came to 310. The name Shafi Khanoum hung tacked to the door on a small card.

He knocked on the door and waited. No sounds from inside. He knocked again and leaned his head toward the door, listening for footsteps. Out of the corner of his eye, he saw two men walking toward him. Justin stood aside to let them pass through the narrow space. He leaned back toward the door and listened again. Barely reflected in the dull-brass door knob, he saw an arm raised at an angle above his head.

He ducked just before a heavy club struck the wooden door where his head had been. The noise resonated down the hall. Before Justin had time to register what was happening, a man pulled the club back up into attack position. Justin reached up, grabbed the man's arm and quickly twisted it until the club fell from his hand to the floor, but another arm tightened around Justin's throat from behind, pulling him backward in a stranglehold.

With both hands Justin reached up to pull at the arm around his neck. It didn't budge. Struggling to maintain his balance, he managed to kick the side of the first man's head as the man reached down for the club in front of Justin. The man fell backwards but recovered quickly. As Justin struggled to remove the arm from around his neck, he felt a strong blow to his stomach.

He saw black. A fist hit him below the eye.

He gasped for breath. Fear turned to rage as thought gave way to instinct. He kicked again at the man in front of him. As the man took a step backward, Justin jabbed his elbow into the ribs of the man behind him. He felt the grip around his neck loosen and took advantage of the moment to reach back and grab the man's jacket. Justin dropped his knee to gain leverage and flipped him forward over his shoulder. The man sprawled across the floor.

In that instant the other man lunged toward Justin in an attempt to grab him by the hair. Justin jerked backward, and the man's own body momentum carried him forward and off balance. Justin had never been in a real fight, and his only experience in hand-to-hand combat was on his high school wrestling team, where he had been an average wrestler, too tall and too skinny. Justin leaped at the second man, grabbing him by the face. As the man pushed against Justin's forearm with both hands, Justin attempted a powerful kick to the man's groin. He heard a deep groan. The man backed off and crouched over in pain.

The man on the floor took advantage of that moment to rise up and take a good swing with his right. Justin managed to block the force of the blow with his left arm, but it grazed his left brow.

Adrenaline pulsed through his veins. He swung back with his right but the man dove for his legs, attempting to throw Justin off balance. Justin stumbled backward as the man hit the floor. Regaining his own balance, Justin kicked hard into the man's ribs. He heard something crack.

The crouching man moved swiftly toward the first, spoke to him in a language that Justin could not identify, and pulled him up. Without looking at Justin, they turned and hastily moved toward the exit, each man bent in pain. Justin took three or four steps in pursuit but stopped. He was breathing heavily and stood stunned. He heard their footsteps grow distant in the stairwell and leaned against the wall to catch his breath. His stomach ached and his eye throbbed. He was furious and afraid.

This was the first time he'd ever been attacked. He had gotten the better hand, mainly because of his size. That, and the months of running and working out were paying off in an unexpected way. He straightened, still panting, knowing that he could not stay there long.

He made his way back down to apartment 310, his hand on his stomach. He knocked again and there was still no reply. He reached down and tried the door handle, silently thanking its semi-reflective surface. The door gave way freely, so he pushed it open just enough to step inside.

The apartment was completely empty; not even a light bulb hung from the ceiling's fixtures. *So much for Marché Transport and Shafi Khanoum,* he thought. They had apparently both vanished into thin air.

That left Romania.

★ ★ ★

Back at the airport, Justin found a public telephone and dialed Stefan Von Portzer. Von Portzer suggested a change of plans. Minutes later, he ran to the Air France desk and changed his ticket for the second time in one day.

The flight would be boarding soon, but he had to hear Gloria's voice. He went back to the row of telephones and dialed her bank. He realized he needed to get a mobile phone.

Gloria answered, "La Caixa."

Her voice lessened the throbbing in his stomach. "Hello, beautiful. It's me, Justin."

"Are you calling from Barcelona?" she asked.

"No. I'm at the airport in Paris." He felt the swelling below his eye.

"In Paris. What are you doing there?"

"It's a long story—related to the audit. I'll tell you all the details when I see you this weekend." He doubted that he even had all the details.

"Will I see you in Barcelona?" she asked.

"Yes, for certain. I'll fly there tomorrow."

"I will be so happy to see you."

"Me too." From the bottom of his heart he wanted to be with her. He looked up to see the number of his flight flashing.

"Gloria. I need to go catch a flight. It's starting to board."

"A flight?" she asked.

"I'm going to spend the night in Zurich and then fly to Barcelona tomorrow."

This caught her by surprise. "You are really getting around."

"I have an old friend from Switzerland who I've not seen for almost a year. We have an opportunity to meet, and I need his advice."

"Justin, are you OK?"

He answered honestly. "I'm really not sure."

★ ★ ★

"Did we get a video of him?" Louis Abdouelle asked.

His secretary sat behind her desk holding a small round mirror in one hand and applying lipstick with the other. She took her time and said, "It didn't work."

"What do you mean it didn't work?"

"Just what I said. It didn't work."

"I paid good money to have that thing installed." He had arranged to have a small camera mounted in the corner of his office ceiling. It was connected to a video recorder in his secretary's office. Right now he was wishing she were not his secretary.

He looked at the machine. "You didn't turn it on. That's the problem. I told you to turn it on whenever there is anyone in the office with me. I want photos of the people who visit me.

"It was a technical error," she said, looking in the mirror, straightening her hair.

"Get the video company out here. I want the activation button installed in my office!" He walked back into his office and slammed the door.

CHAPTER 22

Stefan Von Portzer was sixty-two years old but looked fifty. He slept late in the morning and brunched in the best cafés in Geneva or Vienna. While other people had already started their office routines, Von Portzer would be reading newspapers, reflecting on world events, and strategizing.

When in Vienna, he appeared at his office around one o'clock in the afternoon. His secretary would have his documents ready on the desk in his private office. On arrival he would shut the door, forbidding interruption for one hour. Then, from three o'clock to six o'clock, he would be on the telephone, keeping his contacts and making business deals.

A master of business relationships, the Swiss native had worked during and after the cold-war political climate, forging relationships with the new generation of Eastern European diplomats, bureaucrats, politicians, and opportunists. He had seen the shift from enemies pounding shoes on tables to friends pounding shots of vodka in the dachas around Moscow, and he remained on a first-name basis with leaders from the former Soviet block.

After his office hours, Stefan visited various cocktail-bars, mingling and negotiating. Around ten o'clock, he would join business associates for fancy dinners or attend concerts with friends. Vienna had a richer cultural life than Geneva, but Geneva was where the money flowed. Rumor in both cities had it that Von Portzer employed investigators with inimitable skills to provide him with all manner of information.

But no one really asked. He always delivered, and that was what mattered in business.

At the moment, Von Portzer was en route to the airport from his Geneva apartment. He had been pleased to hear Justin's voice on the phone, but Justin's condensed account of the past seventy-two hours prompted Von Portzer to suggest a meeting in the Zurich airport. Too late to catch the direct flight to Vienna from Geneva, Von Portzer would have to wait in Zurich a couple of hours for his connection. If Justin took the next flight to Zurich, they would arrive at about the same time and have an hour to talk privately.

Besides Charles Graves, Stefan Von Portzer was one of the few people in the world who had stayed in contact with Justin. Chantal's death had been a shock to Stefan. He thought of Justin and Chantal as his protégés, and he had told Justin that if he needed anything, he was there to help.

In fact, Stefan Von Portzer was the only person who could help Justin now.

* * *

Justin followed his instructions and boarded his second flight of the day. The aircraft arrived about fifteen minutes after Von Portzer's, and Justin made his way to the First Class Lounge. He scanned the lounge area and spotted Von Portzer alone at a quiet corner table away from other travelers. Von Portzer was dressed in his typical style, a conservative Viennese jacket and a green overcoat that he had draped across the seat next to him. On top of the jacket lay a green Austrian hat with a feather on the side. Von Portzer looked up from a French magazine and stood to shake Justin's hand.

"Justin. I am happy to see you." Von Portzer greeted him warmly, his accent a strange mix of Swiss- French and Viennese-German.

"Thank you for arranging this," Justin said, relieved to see Stefan.

"Your skin has browned. Be careful in that Spanish sun."

Justin smiled, used to his friend's eccentricities, and waited for Stefan's invitation to sit, even though they were in a airport lounge.

"Please sit down," Von Portzer said, and motioned for the waiter. Ordering two coffees, he took his chair again and leaned forward. "You know, Justin, I have still not recovered from the loss of our beloved Chantal and little Sophie. My heart is very heavy still. How is yours?"

"Better. I think I have gotten over the worst of the pain, but I don't know that it will ever go away completely."

"It is true. Scars remain."

The waiter returned, placed a coffee in front of each of them and disappeared. "Speaking of wounds," Von Portzer continued, "your eye is quite swollen. What has happened to you?"

Justin explained his last three days, concluding by bringing out the papers he had photocopied and handing them to Von Portzer. Stefan sat silent for some time, studying each document and copying details for himself on a small notepad. He sipped his coffee and looked up.

"You say the shipment came from a company in Romania?"

"Yes, here it is: 'Lokomotiva Bucharesti.' And here's the address of the company and details of the shipment. My search for Marché Transport was unsuccessful, but I would still like to find out what that shipment consisted of. Do you think I should go to Romania?" Justin's body tensed a bit.

Von Portzer swished his coffee, allowing it to reach the rim of the cup but not spill over. "Getting the information will not be easy," he began. "In some cases it is still difficult to move freely in Romania without raising suspicions. I know these kinds of places and I have contacts there. I will see what I can do."

"I was running out of ideas. That gives me some hope."

"Don't worry, Justin. I have a reliable source. It may take several weeks, but we will find out more details about that shipment. It sounds like your Marché Transport has just disappeared. If this 'Lokomotiva Bucharesti' company in Romania has not seen the same fate, then at least we have another thread to go on." He watched several travelers walking past and said, "There is also another channel."

"But the only real lead we have is this electronics company in Romania."

"Justin, sometimes you have to look at the road map going out from two directions in the city and sometimes you have to look in the city itself. In this case you have looked at the road to Paris and the road to Romania, but you have forgotten another road, in actual fact a small trail, but one that might be followed."

"Ah, some underground trail, perhaps?"

Von Portzer merely smiled. "My friend, you have known me for six or seven years and we have done successful business together. I trust you have understood that my business relationships vary extensively." He looked away and then back. "One man who occasionally works for me lives near Geneva and is an expert in …" Von Portzer paused, "… research. Market research. I trust this man, and I have used him for several years now. He is young but competent and works with utmost discretion. He may be able to conduct a search in another direction. Where do you fly next?"

"I was going to spend the night here in Zurich and go back to Barcelona tomorrow. It's too late now to catch a flight; I'll book one in the morning."

"If I might suggest something, you still have time to catch the last flight this evening from Zurich to Geneva." Von Portzer reached into his jacket and pulled out a small telephone book. From it he wrote out two telephone numbers and said, "Call the first number only when you get to Geneva; I need to call first. The second number is for a hotel there, the President Wilson. It's by the lake in the middle of the city."

Justin took the paper, looked down, and saw the number, nothing more. "What is it?" he asked.

Von Portzer smiled. "Just call. He may be able to help. I will tell him that you're coming."

Justin decided not to push it. He knew Stefan kept his contacts confidential.

But Stefan changed the subject anyway. "On the telephone you mentioned meeting someone new in Spain." He did not even pose it as a question but expected an answer.

Justin's brow unlined and he sat back in his chair. "She's a green-eyed angel who happens to teach Spanish very well." Describing Gloria relaxed him and made him look forward to Barcelona with fervor. He went on for a while, finally asking, "Do you think I'm moving too fast with her? It hasn't even been a year since losing Chantal, yet we have spent a lot of time together and we get on well."

"Do you love her?"

"Yes, I do," Justin said, without hesitating. "She is different than Chantal, but something about her is similar. What can I say? How do we explain love?"

"Justin, my advice is that you move fast. Take her before somebody else does. One part of your life came to a tragic end, but don't let that stop you from getting the most from the future. I have worried for you, and this now gives you a new chance. If you love this woman don't waste time. She probably needs your love, too."

"I have always appreciated your advice. You know it would be nice to see you in Spain. Why don't you plan to take a few days off and visit me on the Costa Brava? We could drive down to Barcelona together. It's not the same as Paris, but I think you would enjoy the good restaurants and interesting art—Gaudi, Dali. But then, I'm probably telling you what you already know."

"Yes. I was there a couple of years ago and I would like to go again. Now it seems I have an excuse. To go and meet this new lady of yours, that is."

"Just remember," Justin laughed, picturing any number of Stefan's glamorous paramours, "She's mine."

Stefan Von Portzer smiled. He looked up at the monitor on the opposite side of the room and without a word got up and walked to it. His flight for Vienna was flashing. Justine saw Von Portzer take out his cell phone, dial a number and then speak with someone.

Von Portzer returned to Justine, sat down and said, "The market research man is available to see you tomorrow. Call when you arrive in Geneva. He will tell you how things will work from there." He then reached into the inside pocket of his jacket, removed his cell phone again and dialed a number. After no more than two minutes, he turned the phone off and said, "The Hotel President Wilson. They have a room for you."

CHAPTER 23

Stewart-Graves occupied the entire top floor of a stately building in London's financial district. The windows were now dark. They were refurbished originals, their latches more elegant than modern security locks—but far less secure.

Three men waited outside in a rental car.

From what they could tell, the entire building was empty except for the entrance guard.

Yass and Turk made their way around the back of the building to the fire escape. They carefully and quietly climbed upwards floor by floor, moving slowly.

Reaching the top floor, they began to test the windows. Yass balanced himself along a small ledge, inching his way from window to window until eventually he found one left unlatched. He squeezed through a narrow opening, widened it, and signaled to Turk who made his way after him.

They found themselves in a small office with a modern desk and a computer.

Valentine remained in the car, keeping watch on the street. His cell phone was in his hand and he was ready to use it.

Yass and Turk began searching. They needed to find a report headed for a company called Unipac. That was their first objective. Second was to obtain the address of a Justin Collins—someone Ziginiglou had deemed 'insignificant.' Still, *Le Patron* wanted that information.

When Ziginiglou had described this mission and mentioned '*Le Patron*,' Yass had come to attention. Few of the people who worked for *Le Patron* knew his true identity. Yass knew his real name, which made him part of a select inner circle that was tightly controlled and monitored. Once you were in it, absolute loyalty was expected. Yass had no problems with this. The money was good.

From the small office they made their way out into a corridor with offices on each side. Turk whispered, "Where shall we start?"

Yass put his finger to his lips and then motioned for Turk to follow him. They had not been through the entire office and could not be completely sure it was vacant. Yass went to the end of the corridor looking for the managers' offices.

Ziginiglou said the information was sensitive, so it was likely in Mr. Graves' office. Graves had organized the audit in Amsterdam. Yass thought of Amsterdam and the pleasure of knocking the big fat man into the water.

The two men walked down the dark corridor with penlights, inspecting nameplates. They came to a waiting room with overstuffed chairs and a polished mahogany desk arranged with flowers and a computer. Several steps behind the desk, doors led into two different offices.

Yass motioned for Turk to keep a lookout down the corridor, and he inspected the desk drawers one by one.

The secretary was orderly, but he could find nothing with the name of Unipac. He entered the office of Charles Graves while Turk continued his watch. On one side of the desk stretched a long table with several small stacks of papers and binders.

Yass swiftly glanced through them. Instead of Unipac, most of the papers had the name of EuroVinco Corporation on them—audit reports for various factories and entities dealing with that company. This interested Yass. He had reason to believe that some of the people working for *Le Patron* had affiliations with EuroVinco Corporation. Even Ziginiglou ran a department associated with it.

But still none of the material on the table resembled the Unipac report they were after.

Turk came to the door of the office and asked, "How's it going?" Yass moved his finger back and forth to signal that nothing had been found and again motioned for Turk to be quiet. He then pointed to the waiting area. Turk returned to his lookout.

Yass entered Neil Stewart's office and started with a pile of envelopes and papers in a small rectangular tray labeled 'in-box.' On the top of this pile of papers he found what he was looking for. A large yellow inter-office envelope with 'Confidential' rubber stamped next to the name Stewart.

The thick envelope was held shut by a single burgundy string. Yass tugged at it and pulled out the contents far enough to see the title. "Confidential Report for Unipac: Findings of Audit of the EuroVinco Corporation and Recommendations." Paper-clipped to the report was a hand written note: "Neil, here is the final report for Unipac. Will discuss it with the CFO tomorrow. If you have any comments or think we need to make any changes, please let me know. Best regards, Charles."

In the corner of the office stood a small photocopy machine. He signaled to Turk, handed him the report and pointed to the photocopier. The machine was automatic but slow, and Yass estimated that it would take at least ten minutes to photocopy the full one hundred and fifty pages of the report.

While Turk started photocopying, Yass returned to Graves' office to look for the second piece of information he had been instructed to obtain. Ziginiglou had told him that it was Graves who had sent the fat man. It was likely that Graves might have the address of Justin Collins.

It did not take him long. Inside the first drawer of the desk he found a printed list of telephone numbers. Stuck to it were a number of yellow Post-it notes with hand written telephone numbers. One note read, "Call Justin Collins at Bar des Pescaderos, Port de la Selva." A phone number had been scribbled below it. Spanish country code. As Yass wrote down the information on a piece of paper, he heard movement in the outer office. He quickly returned the list to the top drawer and positioned himself behind the door.

The main light flicked on and he heard quick movement across the room. A surprised male voice demanded, "What are you doing here?"

⋆ ⋆ ⋆

Three cities in one day, Justin thought while his aircraft flew in low over dark Lake Geneva, tilted to the right and started its quick descent toward the airport. To his left, the city lights reflected on the water.

Justin was weary. This was how it had been working for Vine Industries: hopping from city to city with very little sleep.

He was familiar with Geneva. Internationals constituted fifty percent of its residents. The real heart and politic of the city, however, was in the hands of the reserved '*bourgeoisie*'—proud Calvinist families who had controlled the city since the time of the early Reformation.

Once the hub of Protestantism, it was obvious that with the number of banks per inhabitant, Geneva's religion was now money. Justin's stockbroker resided here, and he wondered if he would have enough time to make a visit.

After passing customs, Justin bought a calling card and went to find a telephone. Although it was after eleven, he called the number Von Portzer had given him, noticing that the prefix was France. After ringing three times, he heard the line transfer to another. Just as Justin thought he should hang up, he heard a short beep and then a recorded message: "Mr. Collins, you are confirming that you are in Geneva. Please take a taxi to the hotel where you have reservations, and I will contact you tomorrow morning." There was a click and the line went dead.

Justin looked at the phone before placing it back, as if it would offer some explanation. He wondered just what he was getting into, but he trusted Von Portzer.

As instructed, he took a taxi to the Hotel President Wilson. He checked in and took the elevator to his room. After setting down his luggage, he sat on the edge of his bed. Not tired enough to sleep, he also felt that every thought he'd had over the last week was whirring through his head. Declarations of love, odd audits, assaults in dark passageways, and mysterious contacts. It was enough to give him insomnia.

He decided to walk along the lake.

After a while, he found himself wandering through the old town. Its streets were full of young people, and he followed the flow of them to a small square, the '*Place du Bourg de Four*,' which was packed with students drinking beer on the pubs' terraces.

Justin sat down and did likewise. He drank half of his beer quickly and then nursed the rest, remembering his own student days. He had missed much of the social life of college. He supposed that as compensation for the loss of his parents, he had driven himself to succeed, to fill whatever hole their deaths had left in him. But when he met Chantal, he realized that nothing could substitute a close relationship. They had touched souls. When he lost her…well, it was only since meeting Gloria that he had been able to feel he even had a soul again.

Von Portzer's words rang in his ears. *One part of your life came to a tragic end, but don't let that stop you from getting the most from the future.*

The beer was going to his head. Had he forgotten dinner? He vaguely remembered a bag of plane peanuts.

He paid his bill and returned to the hotel in a sleepless exhaustion. With nothing to read, he looked at the nightstand next to his bed and found a Gideon Bible. Justin rarely read religious literature, but he picked up the book, closed his eyes, then randomly opened it and his eyes at the same time. He was looking at a book called Joshua and a couple of lines that said, "Be strong and courageous. Do not tremble or be dismayed, for the Lord your God is with you wherever you go."

"Are you serious?" he asked out loud of the bed lamp, as if it had mis-lighted the passage.

CHAPTER 24

A security guard faced Turk saying, "You don't belong here." Turk just stood there with a silly smile under his large black mustache.

Yass saw the guard sense movement behind him and turn to see what it was. Too late. Yass already had one arm wrapped about the man's neck. With his other hand he pushed on the guard's head and twisted until he felt a snap. The body slumped to the floor as Yass let go.

Yass looked up at Turk who was smiling even wider and said, "Broke like a pencil." Another infidel sent to hell.

Turk finished the photocopying, the last stripe of green light sending shadows up his arms. He returned the original report to the yellow envelope while Yass made a call from his cell phone.

Valentine immediately answered and said, "What's wrong?" Typical Valentine, always expecting the worst.

"We have a little problem," replied Yass. "Drive the car around to the back door of the building and wait there."

"OK, but I don't like changing plans," replied Valentine.

"I don't care what you don't like," Yass growled. "Go now."

The two men looked at each other. Neither uttered a word. Yass took the copy of the report from Turk. They lifted the dead man and carried him out of the office, looking back to make certain nothing had been disturbed. In silence they moved down the corridor to the elevator. Yass assumed there was only one security guard in the entire building, but they had to play it safe, so they took the elevator down to the basement and then found their way up a flight of stairs and out a side door, all the time weighted down with their heavy load.

Outside the entrance Valentine waited with the car. He shifted his head and eyes from one position to another as though he was looking for hidden ghosts in the shadows of the street. The back street was quiet. They opened the trunk of the car and placed the body inside.

Yass took over the driving, not trusting Valentine who might run a red light or get caught for speeding. They could not afford any brushes with the law. He took out a map of London supplied by the car rental company and drove one hour east of the city. At a deserted spot along the Thames, they stripped the body of its clothing and dumped it into the river.

They arrived back in London at four o'clock in the morning, found a large waste bin, opened one of the trash bags inside, emptied it, and stuffed the man's clothing inside. From there, they found a place to park the car on a quiet street and waited another hour in silence. Yass drove his two associates to the train station and then returned the car to a nearby agency.

Two hours later they were in different compartments of a train heading through the Chunnel, between England and France. By noon, they were in Paris, taking a taxi to an address near the Gare de Lyon—an address given them by Ziginiglou.

Yass knocked on the door. Ziginiglou opened it and looked in turn at Yass, Turk, and Valentine, then beyond them to see if anyone else was around.

"You got the report?" he asked.

"*Mais oui*," Yass replied, not breaking eye contact.

"And the address of Collins? Did you get it?"

"*Oui.*"

Yass handed both to Ziginiglou. He accepted them without smiling, then reached into his pocket, removed a thick envelope and held it at

Yass. Yass looked inside at a thick stack of Euros.

Ziginiglou spoke. "Spiros called this morning and said you might be needed again soon. He said you should take the first TGV to the South of France and check in down there."

Yass was tired and was hoping to spend time in Paris. But he felt the stack of euros in his pocket and broke the news to Turk and Valentine. The three of them walked a few blocks to the Gare de Lyon where they boarded a TGV headed for Nice.

Almost immediately upon departure from the train station, both Turk and Valentine were asleep. Yass didn't relax so soon. The train glided toward the Rhone River, passing French fields vibrant in yellows, greens and browns.

Yass only paid attention to the fields insofar as imagining hoards of warriors on horseback riding across them, conquering this land for their faith. When he did drift into sleep it was to his uncle's war dream of killing infidel men and taking their women.

* * *

Friday morning, Gloria Montalvo-Butler made her way to La Caixa bank at seven, two hours before it officially opened. Antonio, the assistant manager opened the door to let her in.

"*Bon dia*," she said in Catalan.

"*Bon dia*," he replied. "I think we will have a busy day with this fiesta. I like celebrating this saint."

"Yes," was all Gloria said. She had forgotten which saint and felt foolish. Too many things on her mind. Here she was considered the good Catholic, yet it was financial-minded Antonio who knew which saint was being honored today.

He smiled and said, "We need to make sure we are prepared. Could you double-check our cash position?"

"Sure," she said as she put her handbag in her desk drawer and made her way to the large walk-in safe where they kept their deposits. Antonio headed with a bag of Euro notes to load the cash machine. After a few minutes, she came back to the lobby for a cup of water.

"Ah Antonio, what would banking in a tourist town be without a cash machine, an ATM as the Americans call it?" Gloria shook her head, filling a paper cup from the water cooler.

"We would go crazy. Good thing you've been here six months already and know your way around—we're going to be crazy even *with* the machine."

She stood there sipping her water, not returning to the safe. Antonio turned toward her. "You don't like routine counting, do you? I can tell. You like to work with people."

Gloria smiled at him. "You read my mind. But it's part of the job, right boss?"

He tilted his head a bit and asked, "Are you liking this part of the training program? I know Llanca isn't exactly Barcelona." He looked out the window. "Well, I guess it's more like the middle of nowhere."

"No," Gloria was quick to say, "It has been good here. I have more time for myself." And someone else, she thought, smiling.

Antonio noticed the dreamy look that settled on her face. "Have you heard from Justin?"

Gloria did not even notice that she had been so transparent. Her thoughts were with Justin and she simply nodded. "I'm meeting him this evening in Barcelona."

Antonio nodded. "Then why don't you leave the bank when we close at one? There are enough people here to finish off the paper work. And you did come in early."

"Thank you, Antonio."

"No problem," he said, turning back to the cash machine. "I wouldn't want Justin to get behind in his Spanish lessons."

CHAPTER 25

The telephone next to Justin's bed rang. It felt like the middle of the night, but the clock on the nightstand said six-thirty. He picked up the telephone, glad that he did not drop it for once. "Hello?"

A voice said, "Please check out of the hotel in thirty minutes and start walking along the promenade toward the center of Geneva on the lake-side of the road. What color is your bag and what are you wearing?"

"My bag is gray," Justin answered, "just a gray airplane carry-on bag, plus a black brief case, and I'm wearing a dark gray business suit."

"Start walking and I will contact you."

The phone went dead and Justin headed straight to the shower. Adrenaline woke his tired body, and he showered, shaved, and dressed in minutes. As instructed, he checked out of the hotel in half an hour.

The lake was right across the street from his hotel, so he started to walk toward central Geneva. Despite being early morning, it was already warm. Large seagulls circled over the lake and white sailboats floated in the harbor. Bright flowers bloomed in patterns around the trees, and the emerald-green grass lay evenly cut around them.

Justin wanted to step out of this tranquil façade and tackle the growing conflict building inside of him. When he neared the Pont du Mont Blanc, the bridge crossing over the Rhone River at the end of the lake, a black Mercedes Benz pulled up to him. The front door opened and a man called out, "Justin Collins?"

"Yes," he answered.

"Please get in."

* * *

Just after seven o'clock, a flight arrived in Bucharest, Romania, and a large blond haired man in a black leather jacket handed his Czech passport to a customs officer who looked at it and handed it back.

Laszlo Vartek, the blond man, noted that things had certainly changed over the years. Years ago it took people hours to get through customs in Bucharest, between the questioning and meticulous luggage searches. A large bill passed from palm to palm had been the way to guarantee entry. Now it only took a minute and no money.

He pulled a slip of paper from his pocket and looked again at the address for Locomotiva Bucharisti. The Swiss man had told him to find information there about a shipment of electronic parts that had been aboard an airplane that crashed on August fourteenth of the previous year.

It was early Friday morning and Laszlo had a choice of either going straight to the factory or to the director's home. He decided on the latter; it might be a better tactic to talk to the director before entering the busy plant.

He took a taxi to the director's home address, about twenty minutes from the airport. The taxi left him in front of a cluster of fifteen gray rectangular apartment buildings. Laszlo looked at the water-stained concrete walls and the ill-kept grounds. Questionable-looking electrical wires ran into some windows.

The morning was still relatively quiet. Exhaust fumes from oxidized cars and rusty buses started to fill the air. Several people left their apartment blocks dressed for work. He headed into one of the blocks and found the name Mircea Cornesceau. He climbed the stairs to the third floor and knocked on the door.

A man dressed in a wrinkled business suit came to the door, opened it several inches, and looked out at Laszlo.

Laszlo spoke in Romanian, "Hello, Mr. Cornesceau?"

The man nodded.

"My name is Moraru." A common Romanian name. "I apologize for bothering you at this time of the morning, but I'm wondering if I could ask you for some information."

Cornesceau waited a moment, looking Laszlo up and down. He then nodded again and led Laszlo into a spacious, well-furnished apartment. It was actually three apartments connected by doors knocked through the walls. Laszlo found himself in a maze of bedrooms, kitchens, and living rooms crammed with antiques, crystal, and classical paintings.

Cornesceau led him to a simple but new couch where Laszlo sat down. "Mr. Cornesceau," Laszlo asked, "I'm seeking information about the Lokomotiva Bucharesti factory. I know little about it or your products, but I need clarification about a shipment that was made by your factory about a year ago."

Cornesceau replied coolly, "It's not our policy to give information on any shipments made by our factory. I'm sorry, but I cannot help." He started to rise. "Now if you would excuse me, I need to leave for work."

"You don't seem to understand," Laszlo said calmly but with steel in his voice. "I'm here to obtain information wanted by my superiors."

Gravity and fear brought Cornesceau back to his chair as he blinked at the last word. Laszlo sat back, leaving the director to define the ambiguity of 'superiors' as belonging to the government, police, army, or even the new Eastern Mafia. Decades of vague authority hung in this country like a thick, wary smog.

Cornesceau cleared his throat and said, "Tell me more." He slumped back into his chair to listen.

"You are the director of Locomotiva Bucharisti. You have access to all records in your company."

"Everything we have is confidential. We don't give out any details on customers or shipments. That's final. Leave now." Cornesceau got up from his chair, reaching for a cupboard drawer. But before he had his hand inside, Laszlo caught Cornesceau by the arm and tossed him back into his chair. The chair creaked as Cornesceau landed on it, but it held.

Cornesceau sat there slightly shaking as Laszlo reached into the drawer for a small Romanian pistol. Laszlo checked it for ammunition, put the safety on and slipped it into his belt behind his lower back, hidden by his leather jacket.

"I see, Mr. Cornesceau, that you are a collector of quality equipment. My superior will be most grateful for this gift," he said. Laszlo was satisfied to have a weapon now. Because of this trip's short notice, he had not been able to make his usual contact in Bucharest. "I want you to know that my superior is a generous man. He shall reward you if you choose to collaborate."

Cornesceau showed some interest.

"One thousand U.S. dollars for the handover of this information. This will be paid directly to you with no strings attached. A little gift in confidentiality."

Cornesceau sat up straight and stopped shaking.

Laszlo reached into his pocket and pulled a money clip full of hundred-dollar bills from his jacket. He took two and handed them to the director. "Mr. Cornesceau. Here is an advance payment for the information. The rest will come when I have the information needed."

"All right, Mr. Moraru. What is it exactly you are looking for?"

"All I want is information on one shipment made by your company about a year ago: who ordered the shipment, its destination and anything else you may be able to disclose."

"That should be possible, but we will have to go to the factory where the records are kept. We will have to be careful. There is still much surveillance in the old state factories." Cornesceau got up from his chair, put the two hundred dollars in his pocket, took his coat from the hanger next to the door, and said, "Come. We will take my car. But as I said, we must be careful. Unknown people are not appreciated in that area of the city."

Laszlo moved the gun into the front pocket of his coat and said, "Let's go."

CHAPTER 26

The driver kept eyeing his rear-view mirror. Justin said nothing, the *film noir* nature of this meeting striking him as comical. The driver was a few years younger than himself, with short, tousled hair and 50s-style, black-rimmed glasses.

They turned through dozens of small Geneva streets, eventually taking Rue de Lausanne along the lake, past the World Trade Organization, the United Nations, several embassies, and finally out of the city. They merged onto the motorway, and after twenty minutes, the car exited, turned left and started toward the Jura Mountains.

The road grew smaller as it curved through small villages. Just past the village of Arzier, they drove down a narrow paved road until they came to a large clearing in the middle of a forest. A Swiss farmhouse and its attached barn looked out over the fields and vineyards that descended down to Lake Geneva. On the opposite side of the lake rose the Alps. Mont Blanc, the tallest mountain in Europe, towered above the other peaks, white and shining even in the summer.

Two large black German Shepherds came out to meet the car, barking and growling with their teeth bared. They ran directly to Justin's side of the car. Until then no words had been exchanged between him and the man.

At that point the man yelled at the dogs. "Baksheesh. Nitrate. Back off!"

Both dogs immediately went back to the house and lay down on blankets next to a pile of logs. Justin noticed a large barn connected to the farmhouse.

The man noticed the look of curiosity on Justin's face and said, "That is my workshop."

"Your workshop," Justin repeated.

"I'm an inventor of sorts. It helps me with my market research," he replied. "Please come in," he said.

The house smelled strongly of coffee. The young man poured himself a cup and offered Justin some as well. "Why don't we go and sit on the terrace?" he asked, as he walked outside. Justin followed him out. Several newspapers and journals in German and French lay scattered across a small table, along with the Wall Street Journal and a couple of computer and electronic magazines in Spanish and Italian.

"Mr. Collins," the young man said, "My name is Doby. I have, on several occasions, done work for our mutual acquaintance, my client. You need to know that my work is confidential and my clients are restricted to a limited few. I only agreed to see you because our friend insisted. That is about all I can tell you."

What was that accent—not British or American. Scandinavian?

Justin tried to focus. "Well, you are more informed than I am. He told me nothing about you, other than that you may be able to help me." Justin loosened his tie and pulled it out of his collar. "He also said something about you fitting into his theory that you don't always look down the roads going out of the city, but in the city itself. I'm hoping you know what that means."

"I understand his theory. And since we both have no time to waste, I suggest that we get straight to the details of this 'city.' You have been in Amsterdam. We need to find out more about a certain company. How can I help research this company?"

Until that point, Justin wasn't sure of the path Von Portzer had sent him on, but now he understood. He had been chasing information about Marché Transport and the Romanian company, but he had not even thought to find out more about the Specialized Trading Department and how this fit within the EuroVinco Corporation. But how could this Doby help him from a little mountain village?

"I'm not sure I understand exactly what you do," Justin began.

"I am what you would call a researcher," Doby replied. "I study economic trends and find information on different markets and companies so that my clients can make the right investment decisions. You could say I go a little deeper than most market researchers, which makes my information more reliable for my clients. Our friend asked for a complete analysis of EuroVinco, but I will be more effective when I have some specifics."

Doby started questioning him. He was more like a detective than any research marketer Justin had worked with. Doby requested names of banks, suppliers, and the kind of computer the company had used, finally asking, "Did you access the company computer?"

"Yes. As part of the audit I had to check data and a few controls to see how many system managers they had."

"Did they give you a password, or do you remember how many passwords they had to go through to get into the main applications in the system?"

"No, someone else got into the system for me, but it seems that he only used one password."

Doby paused, reflected again, and then asked, "Was the computer networked or did log in to other computers to pass data?"

"There was no permanent connection from what I could tell, but there were transmissions to different companies, including banks. Why do you ask?"

"It tells me something about how much security might be on the system."

Justin reached into his briefcase and handed Doby the three photocopies. Three little pieces of paper that could make such a difference.

Doby continued to ask questions and Justin ended up telling him his story about the plane crash and his eventual move to Spain.

Eventually, Doby said, "I think I have enough to start on, but how can I reach you if I need more details?"

Justin gave him the telephone number of Eusebi's barbershop in Llanca, which reminded Justin that he needed to call Eusebi to see if he had any messages.

"If I need to contact you urgently I will use this number, or I will contact you through our friend. What's your e-mail address?"

Justin cleared his throat. "Sorry to say I no longer have one. I left the corporate world a while ago and that with it."

"I'll set up an e-mail address for you," Doby said. "Can you check it at least once a week? If it's urgent I'll phone this." He waved the Tablet he had used to enter the barbershop number. If it's not urgent then I'll e-mail."

"That sounds fine," Justin answered, then thought again and said, "I don't have a computer where I can access e-mail."

"No computer?" This got a reaction akin to horror from Doby—the first true emotion the man had shown. "It's the best way to reach me."

"No computer," Justin tried not to smile. "But...I think there is a cyber café in the village I live in and maybe I could use that. How do I get an email address?"

"Let me handle that," Doby said, leaning back in his chair. "I'll tell you what I'll do." He wrote something on a piece of paper, handed it to Justin and said, "I will set you up with an email address. And, also, there's your password," he said, pointing to four letters on the piece of paper. "Change it the first time you go online. Check there for your e-mail."

At that point Justin felt like an idiot. For six months he had existed without a cell phone or an email address. Indeed he had become out of step with the modern world.

CHAPTER 27

Laszlo Vartek walked half a step behind Cornesceau as they followed a small, dark street behind the Locomotiva Bucharesti factory. They had parked Cornesceau's car in a dirt lot about half a kilometer away.

Bare and empty windows looked out at them. A few tattered curtains hung in strands from partially boarded frames. The air moved a bit, stirring smoke and dust and the reek of grease with it. Laszlo felt both aversion and familiarity in such places—aversion for this part of his heritage and familiarity with these training grounds.

Some years before, while on assignment for Von Portzer in New York, a street gang had attacked him. Five of them planned to rob him, and the attack had nothing to do with the assignment. They had caught him off guard. He was quick and agile, but with five knives coming at him, he had sustained a deep cut requiring several stitches in one arm. Apart from that, he had come out on the winning side. Practice may not make perfect, but it did keep him in existence.

Cornesceau motioned to Laszlo, and they entered a narrow alley between two buildings. Through a back entrance to the factory, Cornesceau led them into an area of small rooms. The spaces were dark and dusty, full of papers, and appeared to be more for storage than office use. Laszlo looked out a glass window, almost opaque with years of smoke, into the main part of the factory. "What's out there?"

Cornesceau replied, "The factory."

Laszlo glared at him. "I can see that. Tell me how it is set up and what they are manufacturing."

Cornesceau pointed off to the right and said, "That's the main production area over there. We will stay away from that. To one side of it is a large room where the shipments come in and we store all kinds of materials used for the production."

Laszlo noted all materials in his line of vision: metal casings, wooden crates, wires, and small steel pipes of various lengths.

Cornesceau continued talking, voice low, "Over there, beyond the production area, we keep the finished products before they are shipped out."

"What are you making?"

He paused. "Weapons."

"What kinds of weapons?"

"Mainly AK47 rifles. We have a license from Russia to manufacture them. But we also make other kinds of weapons. High-quality hand guns, such as the one you took from me this morning."

Laszlo felt the weight of the gun now in the pocket of his leather jacket.

"In fact, we make the finest hand guns in Eastern Europe."

Laszlo was not sure how this connected to the information Von Portzer needed. Was that all they made? "Finest hand guns, so you say. What else?"

"We make special-order defense material, but come. We must keep quiet."

Cornesceau took him through an unlocked door into one of the adjacent offices. "In this room we keep files for the past five years. What exactly are you looking for?"

"For a shipment made by your factory a year ago in early August." Laszlo gave him the details, including the shipping number.

"Most of our files are in order. It should not take much time to find it."

Indeed, despite the seemingly random stacks of boxes, Cornesceau went straight to one box. He began to remove papers from the inside until he found the one he was looking for.

"Ah, here it is." He fixed Laszlo with a stiff-jawed look. "Now, where is the rest of the money you promised?"

Laszlo again pulled out the stack of money, held it tightly in his hand while examining the shipment document, and then counted out eight one-hundred-dollar bills to supplement the two hundred he had already given Cornesceau.

Content only as long as it took to accept the cash, the director grew edgy again. "We must leave now."

Laszlo replied, "I'm not ready to leave. I need everything you know about this shipment. Everything."

"Listen, Mr. Moraru. We have already been here too long, and I'm starting to become so nervous that I cannot move my fingers any longer. We need to leave. It is acceptable that I'm here, but not you. They would never accept that. We must leave."

Laszlo grabbed Cornesceau by the arm and squeezed hard. "Mr. Cornesceau, we are not leaving until I get what I need, even if it means waiting here all day until all your workers leave the factory."

Cornesceau sighed, "Come to my office, then." Laszlo nodded.

They passed through a narrow hallway and another door into a much larger office. Laszlo ordered Cornesceau to sit in a chair in the middle of the room, his back to the door. Laszlo stood facing Cornesceau and the door, keeping both in his direct line of vision.

"There is really nothing I can tell you about the shipment, other than that it came from this factory."

"Mr. Cornesceau, I think you have more to tell. The shipping document says 'electronic components.' That's rather vague. What were those components?"

"You have to understand something, Mr. Moraru. Years ago this was a very successful factory. We had clients all over the world, governments that were friends of our previous government. With the changes over the past years our exports have gone down tremendously. Occasionally we take orders from some of our old clients, although not as many."

"Now that you have fewer clients, it should be even easier for you to tell me what that shipment was all about," Laszlo said.

"I don't remember," Cornesceau replied.

"Next time you don't remember I will use force," Laszlo stated, his cold blue eyes looking at Cornesceau in a way that said he meant business.

Cornesceau slumped in his chair and said, "It was a special order of quality handguns, a few quality electronic detonators, and some explosives."

"Who was the client?"

"I can't tell."

"Yes you can."

"No, my life is in danger if I reveal this."

"Cornesceau, you need to understand that your life is in danger if you don't reveal this." Laszlo took the gun from his pocket and pointed it at Cornesceau's forehead.

Immediately Cornesceau said, "An interim agent was selling weapons to a select group of governments that were approved by our government's export licensing rules. We always follow the rules, and this was an approved reseller."

"And where was this reseller located?"

Cornesceau stared at the gun. "He has offices mainly in Beirut, Algeria and Tunisia, although in this case the shipment was destined for Paris."

"Why Paris? Wasn't it easier to ship directly to the country concerned?"

"Sometimes we would ship to places in Western Europe. From there, our licensed dealers would distribute to their final destinations."

"And where was the final destination of this package?"

"That we don't know. It was up to the dealer to get it to the client. I don't know if it was Beirut, Algeria or Tunisia. I think it was destined for Tunisia, but I'm not really sure. All we did was ship it to Paris, two boxes full of hand guns, electronic devices and explosives to be used with the electronic devices."

Laszlo picked up the shipping document once again. It listed the shipped items. They probably only filled two small boxes. The real items of interest were the electronic detonators and the primer explosives. This was high-grade terrorist material, worthy of blowing up an airplane or any other target. It was the heart and soul of a terrorist's tool kit. Laszlo could tell that Cornesceau's ethics were to sell to anyone willing to pay the price.

"Cornesceau, I want to know about this company in Paris." The gun had not moved.

"As I said, it was connected with some of the other Beirut companies. Any relationship we had with them was only through intermediaries. The intermediaries pay into our bank account and in this case we moved the goods through one of their preferred shipping companies from Paris, Marché Transport. All we did was take the order and manufacture it as specified. Usually we would ship it in one of our trucks, although in this case Marché Transport picked up the order. Everything was done legally under the inspections and rules of the Romanian government."

Laszlo doubted that, but he didn't want to take the conversation in that direction. He held up the papers Cornesceau had found in the boxes, including the bank payment records.

"Do you have any other shipment records with this company? I want them."

"What do you mean?" Cornesceau asked nervously. "You said that was all you wanted and I gave you what you wanted. It would take me several hours to get any other documents."

"Well, let's take the time. I want the records and I'm willing to pay another thousand dollars for this information."

That lightened Cornesceau's face, but he still seemed reluctant. Nevertheless he led Laszlo back through the small door leading toward the archive rooms and said, "Perhaps there is something else. We had a number of other transactions with this company which might be of interest to you."

As they headed down toward the archive room, Laszlo thought he heard low voices. He stopped for a second and sensed movement approaching from one of the larger rooms. He motioned to Cornesceau to move, but Cornesceau froze in his spot.

Suddenly, close to the door, Laszlo heard something metal fall to the ground—a tool? Cornesceau, hearing the sound, broke out of his paralysis and started running through the door into the larger room.

On the other side of the room Laszo saw two men holding hand guns weapons. He suspected they were guards. They looked in his direction and then raised their weapons.

Cornesceau charged across the room. He grabbed an unfinished handgun off a table and yelled, "Attention! Atten—" Before he finished repeating the word, several shots rang out from an automatic weapon and Cornesceau's body thumped forward to the floor.

Laszlo quickly crouched behind a table as a volley of shots went above his head.

CHAPTER 28

Doby drove Justin to the station in Nyon where he caught a train back to Geneva. There, Justin found a telephone booth and called Iberian Airways, booking the next available flight to Barcelona. The flight left at five thirty that evening. He had four hours to kill.

He then called the bank in Llanca and asked for Gloria, but the young man who answered said she had left the bank five minutes ago to catch the train to Barcelona. He felt her absence doubly, unable even to speak with her on a phone.

Something to eat, then. That would satiate at least one hunger.

Justin crossed to the other side of the lake and to the Place Molard, an open area full of restaurants with outside seating. In July the restaurants were full, but he managed to find an umbrella-shaded table and ordered the Geneva specialty, *filets de perches*. The waiter brought him a plate circled with tiny fillets of perches cooked in butter and served with French fries and salad. He drank a small bottle of Swiss white wine and watched people walk by.

After paying his bill, Justin headed down the Rue du Rhône, a principal shopping street lined with banks and large department stores. Numerous smaller streets branched from this one—exclusive passageways full of jewelry shops where one could choose from a Rolex watch for ten thousand dollars or a diamond necklace for over a million.

Justin had something else on his mind. He looked at the window displays of several jewelry shops until he saw an item he wanted.

When he emerged from the shop, he stood still on the sidewalk for several minutes, holding the small box in his hand and looking up at the afternoon sun, remembering another ring and another woman. He put the small box in the pocket of his coat, and headed for a taxi. Senora Pascual had insisted that he do the right thing, yet doubts still existed in the far corners of his mind.

* * *

Laszlo crouched down behind a metal filing cabinet and carefully lifted his head to survey the room. Some meters away he saw Cornesceau's body lying motionless. Further beyond, he saw the two men in black leather jackets moving in his direction with their guns raised.

One of them said to the other, "That idiot had a gun and was out to kill us. I had to shoot him. Who knows, it could have been a trap." Looking down at the dead body he continued, "That was a good shot, right through the heart. I'm the best shot in Bucharest."

The other man replied, "Drago, you are also the craziest shot in Bucharest. You should not have shot so fast. That's the director of the factory. Yes, he was a pot of garbage. Still, you did not think. Remember we were told there may be a second man."

"If there is," Drago replied, "he is as good as dead—and as dead as this one." They both laughed.

Laszlo, still behind the metal cabinet, would have to get past the two armed men as well as any remaining factory workers. But it looked like the last of them were running for the exit doors of the factory. It was impossible for him to reach a door without being seen.

He heard the man command, "Drago, go look over there. I'll go to the office." He was pointing in Laszlo's direction.

Laszlo crawled from the filing cabinet and hid behind several large stacked crates. From here, he had a better visual angle on the two men who were now moving apart from each other. They are making a mistake, he thought. They should at least cover each other. He reached for the pistol in the pocket of his jacket and held it in his hand, safety off. The two men separating increased his chances of making it out alive.

The taller man, now assuming a leadership role, yelled out, "Drago, what are you doing?"

Drago had stopped by one of the tables where there were about twenty or thirty finished handguns laid out on a table. "I'm taking some guns. They will make good gifts."

"Don't be stupid. Our friends have enough guns. First we search the building."

The other man turned and went into Cornesceau's office. In spite of what he had been told, Drago was now filling his pockets with as many guns as they would hold.

By this point the factory was empty. Drago started to move in Laszlo's direction but got sidetracked by an entire table of handgun parts. He could not resist handling the smooth curved pieces, trying to see how they fit together.

Ex-KGB agents or the Hungarian Secret Police would have never made these mistakes, Laszlo thought. Drago, distracted, moved from admiring the tools on the table and handling the unfinished weapons to searching employee lockers. He went from locker to locker digging through pockets, taking anything of value. At one point he found a pack of cigarettes, pulled one out and lit it. He put the half-empty pack into his pocket, the same pocket that was full of handguns.

The tall man who had entered Cornesceau's office also got sidetracked looking at papers on the desk. Laszlo silently entered the room through the side door and crept up behind him. Startled, the man turned around and raised his automatic pistol, but Laszlo was faster. While Laszlo gripped his opponent's wrist to point the pistol in the opposite direction, his right hand jabbed the man's neck. He felt cartilage give way at the windpipe. The man fell backward and sent a desk lamp crashing to the floor, his body following it.

Laszlo lunged to the entrance of the office. He saw that Drago had noticed the noise and had turned, gun in hand and cigarette in mouth, and was looking at the office door. Drago fired and a bullet ricocheted off the wall close to Laszlo's head. Laszlo pulled the trigger. Drago took a bullet to the chest and his gun clattered to the ground. His mouth gaped open, releasing the cigarette. Laszlo fired a second shot, hitting Drago in the forehead.

Drago fell backwards against a table, sending tools, gun parts, and glass containers sprawling in all directions and onto the concrete floor. Bits of shattered glass flew everywhere and landed in spilled liquids. Within seconds, flames rose from sparked papers and began to spread up the wooden walls.

Laszlo's research here had come to an end. He ran back to Cornesceau's body, reached into the dead man's pocket and pulled out the hundred dollar bills and car keys. His boss had always told him, "Your life comes ahead of money," but when you grow up digging through garbage cans for dinner, you don't let money go to waste.

He left the storage area they had first entered and eased open the exit door that led to the alley. Clear. If anything, the factory workers would have gathered in front of the main entrance. Laszlo moved rapidly down the alleyway and out into the street. He walked as fast as he could to the car without running and started the engine.

The deep blast of an explosion shook the automobile. For a second, Laszlo thought he would die by car bomb. Then he heard a second explosion and realized the sound had come from the factory.

Fueled by gunpowder and countless barrels of explosive materials, the Locomotiva Bucharesti factory proceeded to blast itself into the sky. Smoke ascended and debris descended. Hundreds of people appeared from nowhere, pouring out of other factories and offices to watch the blaze. Flames rose in angry fingers, grasping oxygen and reaching higher.

A less than discreet escape.

Laszlo took a deep breath. No, practice certainly did not make perfect.

CHAPTER 29

Spiros answered the telephone.

The cold voice demanded, "Did you get the information?" *Le Patron.*

"Yes, I have it. Ziginiglou faxed it to me a few minutes ago. It was around one hundred and fifty pages."

"What is the result?"

"Positive. Everything passed. Our accounting was in order. The only scare was the Specialized Trading Department, but nothing turned up in the final report." Spiros knew this news would be well received by

Le Patron.

"So they did not spot any unusual operations?"

"No. Nothing."

"Good. Our accountants shall be duly rewarded."

Spiros knew that several accountants within EuroVinco were in fact working for *Le Patron*, Ziginiglou being one of them. What Spiros didn't know was that the Chief Financial Officer of EuroVinco was also working for *Le Patron*.

It was not uncommon for European companies to have a Chief Financial Officer as the second most powerful person in the company after the Managing Director or CEO.

Most companies also kept four sets of books: one for the shareholders, brimming with optimism, carrying all the credibility of 'transparency' and claims of 'following accounting standards'; a second for management reporting, a set of accounts allowing the managers of the various business units within the company to oversee internal reporting; a third set destined for the taxman, with the company's best interest in mind; and finally, the fourth set of books for the top managers of the company, to be used to redirect money flows for specific purposes.

This fourth set of books gauged the true state of the company. It took either a split personality or a very skilled accountant to juggle the different truths and make sense of everything in the four-volume set.

This particular CFO had devised an intricate accounting system through which transactions could be camouflaged from even the most discerning auditor. In EuroVinco, a select group from key accounting departments worked with the Specialized Trading Department. Several external companies loosely linked to EuroVinco also redirected the flow of money.

Over time Spiros had gathered information that seemed to link together a small clan of people in EuroVinco who worked for *Le Patron*, but Spiros kept his mouth shut. It was *Le Patron* who pulled the strings and *Le Patron*'s chosen people who implemented his wishes. Spiros was certain they were kept well compensated.

Spiros was not an accountant, but he knew that from the outside, EuroVinco was a clean company. Externally, EuroVinco maintained an impressive façade of efficiency and respectability, its accounting system reputedly sound. Spiros knew that in reality, carefully selected accountants within EuroVinco regularly directed a multitude of illicit transfers into private accounts, including Spiros's own. Spiros also knew, however, that most of the cash was flowing into accounts belonging to *Le Patron*. Any outside auditor who jeopardized this structure would be in danger, which is why the fat auditor in Amsterdam had been disposed of.

Spiros thought he understood a good part of *Le Patron*'s plan, but not all of it. "Is there anything we should do now?"

"No. We will just let nature run its course." Spiros did not know that two high level people working for *Le Patron* were already in San Jose setting up as two surveillance engineers.

Spiros was waiting for the right moment to inform *Le Patron* of another piece of news. But there might never be a good moment. "There is just one little problem that came up," he said, holding his breath.

"What's that, Spiros?"

"It concerns our team that went to London. A security guard found them after they had made the entry and they had to, ah, take care of him."

"Are they clean?"

"Yes, as far as we know. They handled the problem, taking the guard out of the office and disposing of him appropriately. They left the situation without being noticed."

"Good. We do not want any disruptions. We have tremendous opportunities in front of us."

"We do?" Spiros's voice almost squeaked.

"Call me next week, unless something comes up."

"OK. Er..." Something else just crossed his mind. "Do you remember the second auditor, a Justin Collins? Our three men found out where he could be contacted."

"Oh, yes. Where does he live?"

"Somewhere north of Barcelona. But there's another thing."

"What?"

"We found out that Collins did not go directly back to Barcelona but went to Paris instead."

Le Patron remained silent, waiting for Spiros to tell him what he knew. Spiros hated when *Le Patron* did that, but he continued, "Well, he was seeking information, but he didn't find out anything. Some of our men in Paris gave him a bad time. He went to the airport and took a flight to Zurich and then on to Geneva, which doesn't make much sense. From there, he is flying to Barcelona tonight. Our computer specialists here in Nice managed to find his flight schedule in the airline databases.”

“I suspect he found something. I want to keep an eye on him. But don’t take any unnecessary measures. Not at this point. Just watch him.”

Spiros thought for a moment, and said, “The problem is that Yass and his team are now on the train coming down to Nice from Paris. We won’t be able to get any of them to Barcelona before Collins gets there.”

“Call our agency in Barcelona and get them to follow Collins once he arrives at the airport. And send one of our people down to Spain. Make sure he stays covert. He can keep an eye on Collins for a few days to watch for any irregular behavior. If our man gets noticed, then pull him out. Do you understand?”

“Yes sir,” Spiros replied.

The line went dead. Spiros hung up the phone. His hands were shaking.

★ ★ ★

Justin stood in front of a bank of airport telephone booths for the umpteenth time in—how long? One day? Two? That familiar and unwelcome traveler’s dislocation of time and place was beginning to catch up with him.

He needed to call…? Gloria. At her parents’ house. He swallowed. The small box in his pocket made large lump in his throat. He dialed the number.

“*Diga-me*,” a woman’s voice answered. It was Señora Montalvo-Butler, Gloria’s mother.

Justin spoke in English, knowing that Señora Montalvo spoke it. He had really better pay more attention to his language lessons. “Hello, Mrs. Montalvo. This is Justin Collins.”

“Hello, Justin,” she said, her voice warm. “It is good to hear from you. Gloria said that you had to go on business in Amsterdam. How are you?”

“Fine, Mrs. Montalvo, and how are you?”

“I’m doing well. It is so nice to have Gloria here for the weekend. Wait a minute, she is here. I will call her.”

In a few seconds Gloria came to the phone. “Hello,” she said.

He could taste her voice. “Hello. Are you well?”

“I am happy,” she answered. “So happy to hear you. Are you already in Barcelona?"

"No, I'm calling from the airport in Geneva."

"Geneva? What are you doing there?"

"I will tell you tonight. In Barcelona. I was thinking we could meet at eight at the Spanish Fountain near Las Ramblas."

"I will be there."

CHAPTER 30

Seven p.m. The Geneva flight made it to Barcelona right on time. A man leaned against an airport wall, watching for a tall man to leave the gate. *American, maybe one meter ninety four or five with green eyes, dark hair, possibly wearing a gray business suit.*

Still watching, he pulled out a pack of Spanish Ducados, put one between his lips and started to light it, but realized he needed to go outside the building. The no-smoking laws had become strict in Spain and he detested the politicians as a result. He did not have to wait long. The man he was looking for emerged, a suit amidst the tourists in hats and sandals.

He followed the man outside the terminal and quickly lit a cigarette. Then he pulled out a phone—smaller than his pack of cigarettes—and made a brief call, his mouth barely moving under his thick black moustache.

* * *

The flight from Geneva had been full. It was the height of summer, and tourists were bound for Spain wearing every color under the sun. Justin felt quite gray in his suit of that color. He headed for the line of taxis and requested the Hotel Princessa Plaza. Gloria had offered for him to stay with her family, but...but what? He wanted to go about this honorably. He had something to ask Mr. Butler. Staying in his home meant possibly running into him or Gloria's mother on the way from the shower or toilet. He was nervous enough about meeting Gloria at Las Ramblas.

After checking into his hotel and changing his suit to include a shirt of deep blue, he set out again. He arrived a few minutes early and tried not to look at his watch. Instead, he looked up toward the Spanish

Fountain. Then he looked down Las Ramblas. No Gloria. *Concentrate on something else,* he told himself.

Las Ramblas was one of Barcelona's mythical streets. Justin watched a vendor sell a parrot, a portraitist position her subject and Brazilian dancers spin from the hip in whirling circles. Catalan families strolled past lovers kissing across café tables. Along this promenade, lunch was served to cultivate business relationships, and dinner was reserved for love.

Justin was here for the business of love.

And suddenly there she was. Men's heads turned to follow her figure in its tailored cotton dress, the evening sunlight soft and silhouetting. She crossed the square, turning her head to look for him, and the memory of her profile made his own face tingle.

She saw him as he rose to meet her. They embraced, each conscious that this was the first time they had been away from each other. A week's worth of waiting passed between them as they kissed.

They said nothing, just stood back a bit and looked at each other, then turned and walked down Las Ramblas until they found an empty table at an outdoor café. Justin's eyes kept wandering to Gloria's red lips. When the waiter came, he almost ordered a kiss instead of the pitcher of sangria and a plate of chorizo.

She took his hand and pressed it against her cheek. It was smooth and soft, blending with the warmth of the Spanish evening.

A street performer started juggling four pieces of fruit near them, attracting a small crowd. As an orange and pomegranate crossed paths in mid-air, a man with a black moustache moved toward the crowd's edge, smoking a Ducado.

The juggler's partner, a magician, produced a bouquet of artificial roses. They disappeared under his handkerchief, and out popped one real red rose. As the crowd applauded, he stepped over and handed the rose to Gloria, winking at Justin.

The crowd thinned, and the man with a mustache took a seat at a table nearby.

Justin and Gloria finished the sangria and walked down to the waterfront. Eventually they came to the end of Las Ramblas, where a statue of Christopher Columbus stood atop a pillar, looking out at the Mediterranean Sea. A half-crescent moon hung above the water, stippling light across the dark surface.

"Gloria." He wasn't sure if he had thought or spoken, so he repeated, "Gloria. I know we haven't been together for long, and I hope that this is not too sudden." He looked up at Columbus and wondered whether the man was looking forward to the New World or back to the Old one. "When I told you I loved you, I meant it. And it meant that I want to spend the rest of my life with you. To share an adventure together."

"Justin," she laid her hand on his heart. "I am ready to share an adventure with you."

They kissed. This time the future passed between their lips in an oath without words.

Some time later, he asked, "Are you getting hungry?"

"You make me too excited to eat. But yes, I am hungry."

"Good, I made a reservation for us."

★ ★ ★

The restaurant looked over Barcelona's port. They lingered over an aperitif of Spanish sherry and a starter of crevettes. By the time the Zarzuela—various sea food cooked in a garlic tomato sauce—came, they had finished exchanging stories of their last week.

After dessert and brandy, Justin said, "I almost forgot something."

"What?" she asked.

"A little something I picked up today in Geneva." He reached into his pocket and pulled out the small box and held it toward her. "Gloria, will you accept this?"

She held the box in both hands and looked at him. Then she looked inside it a long while. Not raising her eyes, she asked, "You're serious?"

"Yes."

She slipped the ring off its mount and held it to the candle light. A two-carat diamond rested in the middle of a platinum band flanked by two smaller diamonds.

"It is beautiful. I would be afraid to wear it."

"I wanted something wonderful for you. But it's true, you can't wear it."

"What do you mean?" She looked up at him now, puzzled.

"Well, you can wear it tonight, but please take it off when you go home. I think I got things out of order and should have talked with your father first. That's the correct thing to do."

"Oh, you mean you want to do the Spanish man-to-man thing. I thought we could just elope tonight," she laughed.

"What do you think your father will say?"

"I don't know. Why don't you ask him tomorrow?" Her green eyes sparkled. "My parents have invited you for lunch." She seemed to relax as the knot in his stomach tightened.

He sat up a bit straighter. "What time do you want me to be there?"

* * *

On Friday after leaving the weapons factory, Laszlo hired a small private plane and pilot who flew him from Bucharest to Vienna—conveniently paid for from the money he had taken from Cornesceau. With the explosion of the Locomotiva Bucharesti splashed about in the local news, Laszlo decided not to risk a commercial flight in the event that someone might recognize him.

In Vienna that evening, he met with Von Portzer at a small bar, debriefing him on the Bucharest events and findings.

"We may have stirred up a hornet's nest with Justin's investigation in Paris and your incident in Bucharest," Von Portzer said, not looking at Laszlo but at the end of his cigar. "Half a city block of industrial buildings blown up sky-high and broadcast on all the evening news channels. Hmm. It is probably best if you rent a car and head to Llanca as Collins's security. Familiarize yourself with the town—he won't be returning till Sunday evening."

Laszlo had the feeling that Von Portzer was concerned for this Justin Collins more as a friend than as a business interest. "Do you have a photograph of the man?" he asked.

Von Portzer reached into a small notebook and pulled out a photo, handing it to Laszlo. "This is Collins and his wife—the one who died in the plane crash we seem to be investigating."

Laszlo looked at a man standing next to a lovely, pale-blond woman at a Parisian restaurant.

"It was taken just before she died," Von Portzer explained, tapping ash into the glass tray on their table, intent on each falling flake of gray. A waitress came and cleared away their empty glasses. When she asked if they wanted anything else, Von Portzer shook his head—whether in reply to the woman or his own thoughts, Laszlo could not tell.

Von Portzer finally looked up at him and said, "Let's try and keep Justin from the same fate."

* * *

The next morning, Justin slept in till eleven, then went in search of coffee. He bought a large bouquet of dahlias for Señora Montalvo-Butler and a box of chocolates for the rest of the family.

Justin arrived on the quiet, tree-lined street and rang the doorbell of the Montalvo-Butler mansion. Gloria's younger sister, Carmine, came to the door. At seventeen, Carmine was already a younger, blue-eyed version of Gloria.

When Carmine saw Justin she smiled. "*Hola* Justin. Mama said you were coming. Please come in." Gloria appeared from the direction of the kitchen and gave Justin a kiss on both cheeks. She was wearing a green dress that fit her so well, Justin had to focus on something else. He looked at her hands. As requested, she was not wearing the ring.

Señora Butler appeared from the same direction Gloria had and shook Justin's hand as he offered her the bouquet of flowers. "Justin. They are beautiful," she thanked him. "Welcome to our home. We are running late with lunch. Why don't you go out in the garden and join my husband in the back yard. Carmine, hide those chocolates from your brother before he finds them and eats them all before the meal."

Gloria led Justin to the garden in the back of the house which was surrounded by trees and shrubs so thick they blocked out the suburban setting. On the patio a large table had been set for lunch under two umbrellas. James Butler lifted up his head from his newspaper, stood and shook Justin's hand. James' accent had been tempered after years of living in Spain, but his 'r's still trilled a bit, rich and unmistakably Scottish.

"Ah. Good morning to you Justin. Come join me. I offered to help the women, but they threw me out of the kitchen. Glorious day. Isn't it? What can I get you to drink—how about a glass of white wine? And tell me how you are doing."

CHAPTER 31

Half an hour and two business stories later, Justin leaned forward in his lounge chair—not an easy move with a glass of wine in one hand and the business article Professor Butler had handed him in the other.

Justin set down the newspaper and simply said, "You have a wonderful daughter."

James Butler shot an eyebrow up—they had just been discussing mergers. He tilted his head toward Justin. "She is very special, but I guess all fathers think their daughters are special. No. You used the right word. Wonderful."

"Professor Butler, I'm not sure Gloria that has spoken with you, but last night during dinner… er… I would like to know what you would think if Gloria and I were to consider marriage."

James Butler smiled and said, "Justin, I don't know you that well, but I have to tell you that I like what I see. Gloria has told me a lot about you. I think Gloria and you go well together. I guess I'm a quick judge of character, but I think you have what it takes for someone like her. I would be pleased to support you as a son-in-law and as a friend."

Justin was surprised by Professor Butler's gracious and warm response. "Thank you, I will do my best."

They both sat there for some moments not knowing what to say. Finally, Butler broke the silence. "And your future. What are your plans?"

"Well, getting your approval was the first plan," he answered, exhaling deeply, and they both laughed. Justin continued, "I have enough resources to keep us independent for quite a while. That will give us time to get to know each other. If she wants to continue with her career, that's fine with me. The audit in Amsterdam got me interested in the business world again, and with my experience I should have no problem getting a job, but I just want to make sure I find the right one."

"Well, I don't want to interfere. But the last time you were here I mentioned that you might like to come down to the university and speak to one of my classes, and behind that is an offer for you to look into our doctoral program."

"I've thought about it. Perhaps this fall you can set a time for me to speak to your students?"

"I'd be happy to. I'll arrange for you to meet some of the professors." He set down his drink. "But work aside—as a good Scot, let me just say welcome to the Clan."

Professor Butler stuck out his hand, shook Justin's and laughed, saying, "I just have to tell you that Gloria already had a little meeting with us this morning and informed us of her wishes. To be honest, I never could say no to that child. I know this is quick, but have Gloria and you talked about dates?"

"Not really. I felt it was important to talk with you first."

"Come on, let's go see how lunch is coming. And by the way, why don't you call me James rather than Professor?"

★ ★ ★

With Roberto—Gloria's twenty-year-old brother—finally located, James Butler set a bottle of Cava on the laden table. He stood and made eye contact with each person, beginning, "I have an announcement. Justin and I just had a serious business discussion about the formation of a new partnership. Mama and I already had a discussion with the other half of the partnership this morning. I'm sure this is a surprise to all of you, but I have the pleasure to announce the engagement of Gloria Montalvo-Butler and Justin Collins."

At that, applause broke out. Señora Montalvo-Butler and Carmine kissed Justin, Roberto shook his hand and James Butler popped the cork. He poured a glass of Cava for everyone, and as they raised their glasses he continued, "To Gloria and Justin. May you have happiness throughout your lives and God bless you. *Salute.*"

Gloria gave Justin a look so deep he blinked. He stood up and said, "I just want to thank Professor Butler, ah, James, for this kind toast and to say that I'm very happy to become part of this family. By the way, last night I gave Gloria a little gift."

Gloria smiled and reached under the cloth napkin by her plate, pulling out the small box that said *"De Favre, Genève, Bijouterie."* She handed it to Justin. He opened it and slid the ring onto her finger, while everyone clapped and fussed happily over it. Everyone except Roberto, who cried out, "Are you crazy to spend that on my sister? You could probably have bought a new computer for the price of that."

Justin replied, "Oh, don't worry Roberto. It's really a fake." There was more laughter as everyone started eating the Catalan Salad. Then the only focus was food. James helped his wife bring large dishes and platters out to the patio. They started with *Merluza a la Planxa*, a typical Mediterranean fish, followed by roasted lamb cooked Mediterranean style and a plate of slice baked eggplant. By the time they got to the *Crema Catalana*, a baked sweet custard coated with caramelized sugar, Justin could not help thinking he was privileged that Gloria was capable of her mother's culinary prowess.

When coffee was finally served around four o'clock in the afternoon,

James said, "We forgot to ask about timing. When should we plan this wedding?"

Gloria spoke. "I have always wanted to get married in September like you and Mama." She nodded at both parents. "That gives us about six weeks, unless we wait a year and that would mean thirteen months. So it is either September this year or September next year. What do you all think?"

Without hesitation Carmine and Roberto chanted, "This year! This year! This year!"

Gloria stopped them with raised hands and said, "OK, you have heard the jury's verdict. It will be this September. In fact, it will be on Friday, September seventh at the Castillo de Peralada north of Figueras. It is already booked."

Justin Collins and James Butler looked at each other with their mouths open. James turned and stage-whispered to Justin, "What did I tell you? She always knew exactly what she wanted. I give up. It's your turn to try and start managing her." At this, Gloria wadded her napkin into a ball and tossed it at her father in mock fury. James tossed it to Justin.

Justin gave it back to Gloria, gently closing her hand around it.

CHAPTER 32

Through a small, pocket-sized pair of binoculars, Laszlo examined the faces of people leaving the train station. He had been drinking coffee and sodas at a nearby bar for most of the afternoon and evening, studying the disembarking passengers from the hourly Barcelona trains.

He focused his lenses on a figure and glanced again at the photo Von Portzer had given him. Yes, that looked like a match: a tall, dark-haired man with a suitcase and—he was with a striking young woman? They were talking and smiling at each other.

Was she an acquaintance? No—she slipped her arm through his, and they walked together in the direction of town. Von Portzer hadn't mentioned anything about a woman. Laszlo checked again to see that he had the right man.

Just before he lowered the binoculars to follow him, Laszlo noticed a man in gray pants and a blue blazer with a thick black moustache.

The man hesitated for a few seconds at a train door, stepping off onto the platform only when all the other passengers were well ahead. The man pretended he was taking his time to light a cigarette, but Laszlo knew the patterns 'watchers' followed. The man was looking straight at the couple, keeping a close eye on them as they went around the corner of the station. That had to be Collins, thought Laszlo, woman or no woman.

As the couple walked toward town, the man hurried over to a small parking lot behind the train station where a car was parked—a Peugeot with a French license plate. Laszlo jotted down the number.

The driver signaled the man from the train, opened the door and got out. The two men spoke briefly, both of them looking in the direction Collins and the woman had taken. The driver was much thinner than the other man. He wore a black leather jacket in the middle of July. His eyes kept shifting from place to place, never looking directly at the man he was apparently working with.

The two men left the car at the station and began to track the couple at a distance.

Von Portzer's second sense had been correct. Justin Collins was in trouble.

Laszlo followed the two men who followed Collins and the woman through the center of Llanca, feeling like he was bringing up the rear of a parade. Eventually everyone reached a large house at the far edge of the village. Laszlo had walked past the same house earlier that day and had noticed its several entrances. It was probably broken up into several living units.

Collins and the woman went to one of the side entrances of the house. Laszlo positioned himself beneath a cluster of tall pines with a good view of them and the two men in the shadows. Completely absorbed in one another, neither Collins nor the woman noticed any of their watchers.

With his binoculars, Laszlo got another look at the woman. She was beautiful indeed—and those green eyes. She smiled at Collins, reached up with both arms, and clasped them around his neck. Collins dropped his bag and placed his hands gently on her waist. He held her close and they kissed long enough that Laszlo wondered why Collins did not go inside with her. Instead, he picked up his bag and headed in the direction of the road that led to the Port and the small house next to the sea.

The two men followed Collins about one hundred meters behind. It was still more than a kilometer to Collins's house. Collins took a side street, past a small locals' bar.

Three men emerged from the bar. One of them elbowed another, gesturing toward the two strangers. He wore a jacket with the colors of the Barcelona Football Club. Another of the men, larger and stocky, resembled that of a rugby player. The latter signaled to his friends, and to Laszlo's surprise, began to follow the two darkly dressed men.

Laszlo was some distance away but with a clear view of what no longer seemed a parade so much as a circus. He watched as the three locals approached the two men from behind. The stocky one pulled out a knife and held it to the neck of the man with the shifty eyes.

Laszlo raised his binoculars and took a closer look. No, it wasn't a knife. It was something different. A barber's razor—sharp enough to slit through blood vessels, windpipe and cartilage in one swipe.

The skinny man's eyes darted back and forth even more rapidly as if someone had set a metronome to a faster pace. The other two men backed the man with the mustache against the wall and frisked him, retrieving a handgun from a shoulder holster beneath his sports jacket. They then frisked the skinny one and found another gun.

The locals worked their way through some English, French and Spanish to see how best to communicate. The one with the razor asked questions. Laszlo could hear their voices but not the words. The shifty eyed man tried to break away, but one of the locals grabbed him from behind. Both of them came crashing to the ground, but the city man's face made direct contact with it. His nose started to bleed down his front, disappearing onto the black of his jacket. The local was back on his feet in an instant and gave him a light, harmless kick. The bloodied man slowly raised himself to his feet and leaned against the wall holding his nose.

The man with the razor spoke to the two strangers loudly, pointing in the direction of the train station. Laszlo heard him say, "Don't come back!"

★ ★ ★

The telephone rang in the early morning, waking Spiros. He said, "Hello. Who is it?"

"Hello Spiros. Screw you."

Valentine. By that time he was awake. "So what's going on? Why you call me so early in the morning."

"You told me to call you once a day."

"Yes, but not at six in the morning."

"Why not? That way I know I can reach you."

"So, do you have any news?"

"Yeah."

"What is it?"

"He's here. Collins is here," Valentine said.

Spiros could tell Valentine was nervous. "Well that's good to know. Is there anything unusual?"

"Yeah. I don't like the guy and I don't like his friends."

"What do you mean?"

"They aren't hospitable. That's what I mean. They got knives and they broke my nose." He paused. "They're gonna pay."

Spiros became alarmed. "Valentine. You don't do anything. Just wait. I will get Yass down there to help you. Wait for him."

"I don't need Yass. He's too bossy. I can do it on my own. I can take care of this Collins guy. You told me to."

"Valentine, I didn't tell you that. I told you to stay low, covert, and if there was any problem, to vacate the place."

"Don't send Yass. I'll just watch the guy. They broke my nose."

"OK, just keep cool," Spiros said. "Keep watching him, but stay out of sight. And keep in touch. Call me twice a day. OK?"

"Whatever."

"Just stay out of sight." Spiros hung up the phone. Big mistake, Valentine. He needed to get Yass down to Spain. Now.

CHAPTER 33

When Justin awoke, he lay in bed, looking out at the soft morning sky. He could feel his body between the sheets and the body that wasn't there. Thinking of Gloria made him want to sing, to swim, to fly. He did the first—and his laundry.

After hanging out all the washed and wrinkled shirts he'd worn during the past week to the chorus of "I've Got Rhythm," he joined Gloria for lunch at La Casa Brasa.

They ordered fish and salad. When the fish came, Gloria cut into her fillet with knife and fork. Justin watched the engagement ring move with her finger. "So, did you get any comments this morning at the bank?" he asked, nodding at the ring with a silly smile.

"No, we are too busy with real work to be distracted by meaningless things like that," she said in her best attempt at sternness.

"Yeah, yeah," he said. "I bet."

She lay down her cutlery and held up the ringed hand. "No, it caused quite a commotion for a Monday morning. I had to tell the news to everyone and receive congratulations for us. In fact, the manager has invited us for a drink and celebration."

"With pleasure," Justin said. "So I guess the news is out and now I will have to face all the smiles and kisses from all the old women in Llanca? And I am sure that Señora Pascual will be one of the first."

"It's all part of the bargain," she said, reaching over to link her ring finger with his.

* * *

That evening, Gloria called to say she would be working late at the bank. Justin decided to go out for a run, having chosen laundry over exercise this morning. He usually preferred jogging early in the day, but occasionally these Spanish sunsets lured him out to the hills, sand and sea. The air tasted different late in the evening. As if all the day's scents and colors that had been steeping in the sun now entered his mouth and lungs with a kaleidoscope of flavors.

This evening Justin tried to stay off the main roads. They were not only narrow but also busy with traffic. Instead, he took a dirt road heading west into the brown barren hills behind Llanca. There was enough light to see where he was going, and the road was well leveled. No worries of rocks or potholes.

He left Llanca, jogging the first kilometer slowly to allow his breathing and heart rate to build up to a steady pace. He picked up his speed at a winding road that climbed three kilometers to intersect with another road that he would take back to the village.

To the west, the last shades of pink started to merge into gray gloaming. Deeper purple and blue striped across the Pyrenees. As it often did, this Catalan landscape reminded Justin of California. Perhaps that was why this place felt like home. Even the language linked it to California with its own rich Spanish heritage.

Looking back over the village of Llanca, Justin saw the tiny lights coming on a few at a time. Somewhere within those lights was his beautiful Gloria Montalvo-Butler, soon to be Gloria Montalvo-Butler-

Collins, depending on how the naming conventions worked in Spain.

After increasing his pace and climbing higher into the hills, he could hear the sound of traffic on the main road that ran from the French border south to the next larger town of Figueras about twenty kilometers away. The dirt road he was on narrowed slightly as it ascended into the steep hill. A rocky embankment rose to his right and another bank sloped downward to his left. The road was primarily used for the occasional truck hauling rocks from the quarries down to Llanca for construction.

As Justin continued his ascent, a car approached a short distance behind him. Justin's shoes had fluorescent reflectors on the heels and his shirt was white. The car would be able to see him. Still, wanting to allow the car ample space to pass, Justin ran well along the left side of the road. He slowed his pace and realized the car behind him was increasing speed.

It was coming straight at him.

If he hesitated for even a second, the car would crash into him, sending him flying far over the small cliff. He dove over the side, feeling the sagebrush scrape against his legs. He fell forward, tumbling through rocks and brush, the steep slope and gravity increasing his body momentum until his head hit a boulder and his limbs lay still.

★ ★ ★

Nine time zones away, on Monday morning in San Jose, Sam Oliver entered Unipac's boardroom. As had been the case for over forty years, the company's board meeting was held in a large simple room in the back of a warehouse.

At Unipac's very first meeting, Sam Oliver and his father did not even have chairs, so they had sat on wooden crates. Ever since, one of those crates had been kept in a corner of the room. Numerous articles in newspapers and business magazines had been written about the famous Unipac warehouse, and it had been used as a case study in various business schools around the country.

A massive oval oak table now sat in the center of the room, and comfortable chairs had long since taken the place of crates. The self-service coffee machine had been replaced several times. But traditions held.

The previous month, two of Unipac's original board members had retired. Randolph Sutter and Karl Schubach had joined the team in their stead—two attorneys who had served on the interim board of Vine Industries. When Unipac purchased some of Vine Industries' business units, these two members seemed a logical fit. Unipac needed people with international experience.

Charles Graves sat ready. Arthur Sigg, CFO sat next to him. Paul Kent, the CEO, was discussing something with a woman who had handed him a paper. Kent signed it and the woman left the room. Eleven reports of the EuroVinco audit—one for each person there—lay stacked in front of Charles.

"Well, gentlemen, let's get started," Sam announced. "Thank you all for coming. As we all know, the main topic today, and one that is of vital importance to Unipac, is the decision regarding a merger with EuroVinco.

"EuroVinco provides many excellent opportunities for Unipac. Most importantly, it provides access to the European market. If we decide to go ahead with it and the merger proves successful, shareholders will see a substantial return. If it proves unsuccessful, Unipac will sustain substantial financial losses and it will take years for the company to recover. We must make the right decision.

"We have several related items to go through before we come to that decision. The first one concerns the special audit of EuroVinco that we requested. Mr. Charles Graves, from Stewart-Graves in London, is here to present their findings. I believe this will be an important component of our decision making."

Randolph Sutter and Karl Schubach set their coffees down and leaned forward.

* * *

Laszlo had been watching Collins all day, and things appeared calm. At sundown, however, Collins emerged from the house dressed in shorts, a t-shirt and running shoes and had started jogging in the direction of the main road. Laszlo was in good shape, but he was not a runner, so he headed for his car, wondering exactly how he would follow Collins.

He watched Collins as he headed across the main coastal road and onto a dirt one heading toward the hills. To avoid being seen, Laszlo drove only part way, then parked and followed on foot.

He assumed Collins was safe up this road, but no sooner had the thought entered his mind than a Peugeot sped past him heading in

Collins's direction. French license plate.

Laszlo broke into a run, racing up the road toward Collins. His muscles felt stiff and his breath came hard. He sprinted to the point where he estimated Collins would be and came around a bend in time to see the car accelerating. The driver's intent was obvious.

It was a ten-meter drop to the bottom of the gully.

As Collins's body catapulted over the side, the car halted to a stop in a haze of dust that rose from under the tires like smoke, diffusing the red brake lights in a filmy gauze.

A man got out. Laszlo slowed his pace so as not to make noise—thankfully the motor was still running. The driver said something, but Laszlo couldn't discern the words. Gun in hand, the driver looked over the side of the bank where Collins had jumped.

The road was narrow. Climbing up the hill, Laszlo found it impossible to take cover, but the lights of the car worked in his favor. He could clearly see the outline of the man in his dark nylon jacket and pants. Laszlo had no weapon but he moved forward slowly, breathing heavily, his heart still pounding from the sprint.

At this point he recognized the man. It was the skinny, nervous one from the night before. He darted his eyes over the small cliff, finally resting them on something—some*one*. He raised his gun. "Good bye, Collins," he called over the edge. "See who protects you now." He took aim.

In an instant, Laszlo moved behind him with one fatal jab to his trachea. The man twisted to the ground, landing face up, eyes finally motionless.

CHAPTER 34

Tuesday morning in Llanca, tourists had already sardined themselves across the beach. Laszlo walked among them, avoiding the spokes of umbrellas and rolling beach balls.

After his long telephone conversation the previous night with Stefan Von Portzer, he now needed a partner, someone who could speak French. He knew who he needed.

The man was a local, so it shouldn't be too hard to find him. The locals hung out together, both in the evenings and during the day. While the tourists spent their evenings dining at the restaurants tucked tightly on the waterfront and getting tipsy in the neon-lighted nightclubs by the port, the locals preferred places in the Old Town. They would gather in small stuffy bars, smoke cigarettes and discuss local politics or the football game that inevitably played on the TV screen above the bar. One of these local hangouts interested Laszlo. The Pacu-Pacu bar. It was always full. And it was the place the stocky man and his friends had emerged from the other night to aid Collins.

He reached the Pacu-Pacu bar and walked in. His eyes took a few seconds to adjust to the dim and smoky atmosphere. Real Madrid was playing against its rival, Barcelona Football Club. It was a replay, but the onlookers reacted as though it were a live match. They supported Barcelona to a man.

Laszlo spotted the one he was looking for. He sat at a table in the back of the bar with the two friends and six other men who ranged in age from about fifteen to seventy. He knew this would be an inappropriate time to conduct business, so he sat down on a stool in front of the bar and ordered a coffee. The coffee came, and he sat watching the game until it ended and the bar occupants cleared out and headed to work.

The stocky man and his two friends were the last to leave. Laszlo went straight up to him.

"Excuse me."

The Spaniard turned around and stared at Laszlo, his two friends standing on either side of him.

"Excuse me. I apologize for approaching you like this, but I think we have a friend in common, Justin Collins. I wonder if I could speak with you about him."

"*No hablo Ingles,*" the man replied.

"Look, I know you speak English and I know this is sudden, but Justin Collins is in danger, and I would like to seek your advice. Is there a place we can talk?"

The man's face remained stoic as he took in Laszlo's looming presence and earnest request. He said, "Come with me."

In front of the Pacu-Pacu was parked an old Renault, just barely able to hold the four of them. Laszlo was told to enter the front seat next to the driver, the one wearing the Barcelona Football Club jacket. The other two sat in back.

They drove through the Old Town and down a narrow street. The car stopped in front of a barbershop, and Laszlo was told to get out and go inside.

Laszlo pushed the yellow curtain aside and walked into the dark room. The man followed. An older man stood next to a chair with a barber's razor in one hand and a cigarette in the other.

"*Hola*," the man with Laszlo said.

"*Bon Dia*," the barber answered.

The stocky man went to a wooden door in the back of the barbershop, opened it, and motioned for Laszlo to walk through.

Laszlo was surprised to find himself in a bright, open courtyard with a fountain in the middle, ornamented with multicolored Spanish tiles. He was led to a shady corner set with a table and chairs. The man motioned for Laszlo to sit down. He then took a chair opposite Laszlo, and as he did so his two friends appeared in the courtyard, each taking up a position some distance away from where the two were seated.

"*Hombre*. Tell me."

"My name is Laszlo Vartek. I have been hired to protect Justin Collins. I believe you can help me."

"Explain," said the stocky man.

"Last Friday my employer met with Collins at the airport in Zurich. As a result of that meeting, my employer believed that Collins might be in danger. This was confirmed on Sunday night when I saw two men following him. They were very effectively taken care of."

Laszlo looked the stocky man in the eye and he thought he saw a slight smile on his face. Laszlo smiled even less perceptibly. "I see you know what I mean."

"Continue."

"Sunday night was not the only problem. Monday night—last night—one of those men came back for Collins and tried to kill him. Collins is now in the hospital in Figueras. I don't know how he is doing, but you can find him there. I think he has a girlfriend and she should be told, unless she knows already."

"Just a minute," the stocky one said, and he called one of his friends over, spoke in Catalan and the man entered a room on the side of the courtyard.

They waited a few minutes in silence. The man came back and nodded his head. The stocky one left the table to speak a few words with him. He returned with a look of concern and asked, "How did he get to the hospital?"

"Someone brought him there." It was Laszlo's turn to be uninformative.

"And what happened to the man who hurt him?"

"He is in a burned car sitting at the bottom of a small cliff on a dirt road leading to one of the rock quarries east of Llanca. It's the same man you talked to on Monday night, the one that had the razor to his throat."

"And how do you know this?"

Laszlo blinked. "I saw it happen."

"And how did the man get into the burned car?"

"Someone put him there."

"Did you see it?"

"Someone did."

The stocky one waited for a minute, then said, "I don't like criminals in my village."

Laszlo wasn't sure he meant the men who followed Collins or himself. "We believe Collins is in danger. I need assistance." He looked the Spanish man in his dark eyes. The Spanish man stared back.

Laszlo waited.

"What is your proposition?" the Spanish man said.

"I saw that you…assisted Justin on Sunday night. But I don't understand why you and your friends did it. What do you stand to gain?"

"Listen, Llanca may seem like a beach where tides of tourists come in and wash out every year, leaving nothing alive after their coming and going. But this town is full of people who want to lead honorable lives. These people are my family and I will do anything to protect them from harm. When *El Americano* came here, I could see that he was in bad shape. He decided to stay here, at first for only a few weeks, then longer. Now he is even marrying a Catalan woman. Out of respect and honor for our Catalan sister, we helped him the other night."

"Do you think that was the end of it?" Laszlo asked.

"It sounds like it wasn't."

"Would you be willing to help?"

"Within reason, yes."

"Then I have a request, a proposal."

"What is your proposal, Mr. Vartek?"

"First, what is your name?"

"My name is Pujols, Jordi Pujols."

CHAPTER 35

Through a hazy fog, several colors circled around the room until they settled on a woman's face, her green eyes tender.

His head was throbbing but he smiled at her the length of a full gaze. Finally he said, "I know this is the cliché question, but what happened?"

"That's what I should be asking you." She poked at him through the white sheet laying across his chest.

"OK, cliché number two: where am I?"

"You are in the Figueras hospital."

He closed his eyes, trying to fit things together and giving up. Instead he reached for her face and said, "You have beautiful eyes."

She smiled. "I thought you were going to sleep all morning."

"What time is it?"

"It's eleven o'clock. I have been so worried about you."

His mind began to clear. "How long have I been here?"

"Around thirty-five hours."

"And how did you know I was here?" His hand met hers as she reached for him.

"At first, the hospital didn't know who you were. They called the *Guardia Civile* in Figueras, and by your description the *Guardia Civile* in Llanca identified you."

"Are you saying I'm infamous with the Llanca police?"

"Oh no. They identified you by your size and the fact that you were wearing a *San Francisco 49ers* t-shirt. I was out, so they called Jordi. He came by the bank last night when it was closing and one of his friends brought me here. I stayed until eleven last night."

Random images of the night before—no, two nights before—passed through his mind. Jogging at sunset. City lights. The dirt road. The car. "I went out jogging. I remember that a car tried to hit me."

"Where were you jogging?"

Justin's mind was spinning. He tried to lift himself up from the bed, but his head pounded and he fell back saying, "My head feels like someone dropped a lead brick on it."

"Justin. You have a concussion. A slight concussion, but it still is a concussion. You need to lie still for a few days. Your ribs are bruised. Thank God you have no broken bones and only few stitches on your head. I don't know how it happened, but I am so happy it is nothing worse."

"Do you work here? I don't think I know you," Justin teased.

"I am just the woman you are going to marry in a little over six weeks." She smiled, sealing the deal with a kiss.

After that, Justin really needed to clear his head. But he tried, "How did I get here?"

"No one knows."

"What do you mean no one knows? Figueras is twenty kilometers from Llanca. I didn't get hit by a car and then jog over twenty kilometers with bruised ribs and a concussion."

"Someone brought you here but disappeared without leaving a name. Maybe it was the person who hit you with his car and did not want to get in trouble. But you were unconscious."

He didn't like the sound of that word. "Well, at least I will get a good rest for a few days."

"Justin. You can't remember what happened? Really?"

"Not really. I need a little time to get my head straight." He paused. "Oh, there is just one thing I do remember."

"What is that?"

"I remember that I love you."

"You are a silly man, and I love you too."

★ ★ ★

Laszlo and Jordi walked down a street near the Gare de Lyon. They had driven to Barcelona early and caught the first flight to Paris.

Laszlo's instincts had been correct. Jordi had certain useful skills that he had picked up from the French Foreign Legion. And since Laszlo only spoke a few phrases in French, Jordi could do most of the talking.

Their objective was to track down the additional information Laszlo had found in the Bucharest factory. He had discussed this with Stefan Von Portzer and it seemed the only avenue left. Other than Doby. Hopefully he would find something through his investigations.

Laszlo knew that Collins had already been to Paris, but they had to try again.

Besides Marché Transport they had the name of a Shafi Khanoum. Justin had told Von Portzer that he had visited an agency near the Gare de Lyon with a link to the man. A Louis Abdouelle ran it.

They eventually found what they were looking for. Twenty-five Rue Augustine. The door was open so they went inside. The reception office was vacant. They walked into a second office and found a man sitting behind a desk going through some papers. The man looked up, surprised.

"Hello, Mr. Abdouelle. We want to ask you some questions," said Jordi, his dark eyes hard. Laszlo shut the door behind them, standing guard, studying Louis Abdouelle with his own impassive eyes.

"Who are you? Get out of here," Abdouelle shouted.

"Quiet. We are here to get some information," Jordi responded.

Abdouelle made a quick move for a drawer, but Jordi beat him to it. With the man's hand in the drawer, Jordi slammed it closed. Laszlo liked his style. Abdouelle yelped and pulled out his injured hand, waving it back and forth in the air and blowing on it.

Jordi opened the drawer and pulled out a medium sized hunting knife. "Did you think this would stop us?" he asked, offended. He frowned at the blade then looked back at Abdouelle. "Now, we have a few simple questions."

Abdouelle sighed and gestured a whatever with his good hand.

"We're here to find out about a company called Marché Transport. What do you know about them?"

"Nothing. You are the second person in a week to ask me about them. There was someone here last Thursday. Are you with him?"

"No. I don't know who you are talking about. Tell us what you know about Marché Transport."

"Funny, they're more popular gone than when they were around. All I know is that someone by the name of Khanoum, Shafi Khanoum, approached me over a year ago. I'm a housing agent and they were looking for office space. I represented them in obtaining office space in Villepinte, helping them negotiate and close a contract. I was paid a commission for my work and that is all."

"That is all?"

"Yes, that is all!"

"Are you sure?"

"Yes."

"Then answer this." Jordi looked him straight in the eye, moving his thumb along the edge of the blade. "Why was your telephone number on a shipping document ordering delivery of illegal explosive devices?"

"I don't believe it," Abdouelle answered.

"We have reason to doubt you." Jordi paused. "Now think hard." He placed one of his own fingers on the table and held the knife over his finger. "Abdouelle, holding back information will have painful consequences." He pulled his finger back and then stared at Louis Abdouelle's hand, still holding the knife in the air.

★ ★ ★

Abdouelle looked at the knife and then at Jordi staring at him, and then across the room at the large blond man who stood there motionless. A bead of sweat formed on Abdouelle's left temple.

"Abdouelle?" Jordi questioned.

"OK," resigned Abdouelle. "It was a misfortune. Somehow I got tangled into a misfortune." He threw up his arms at this. "In France there are many different kinds of gangs and the neighborhood here is rough. Over a year ago a group approached me with a request. I thought it was legitimate. They were looking for a place to set up their shipping company. I did a number of jobs for them and they paid well." The bead of sweat slowly rolled down to his jaw line.

"What kind of jobs?"

"It started with getting space in Villepinte for their shipping company, but then they had me making other kinds of telephone calls, making payments."

"How? Where? What were they doing?"

"This was a group of *pieds-noirs*. It took me some time, but I found out that they were looking for ways to make special shipments to North Africa and other places around the Middle East—shipments that did not pass through customs. Somehow they were working with the Albanians." With the sleeve of his free arm he wiped his forehead.

"What was in the shipments?"

"From Europe they were shipping weapons and explosives to North Africa, the Middle East and Colombia. The return was drugs…and prostitutes. That's where the Albanians fit in. They figured out a way to get things to their clients without passing customs."

"Albanians?"

"Kosovo Albanians. Different gangs. NATO saved their asses from the Serbs and now they turn around and supply most of the drugs and prostitutes into Europe, while NATO is still there protecting them."

"And Marché Transport and the people behind it, who were their clients?"

"As I said, gangs. They are all over the place. The gangs in the Middle East want weapons and explosives. The gangs in Europe want drugs and prostitutes. It was an exchange."

"And how did it work?"

"A very simple and clever method. They would use private corporate jets to transport goods," explained Abdouelle. "They paid off the pilots, and when they flew important people around the Mediterranean, for example, there were additional boxes placed in the cargo areas of these jets. No one knew about it but the pilots, and when the planes landed at private airports there were ground workers who took the boxes." He looked from Jordi to Laszlo and back at Jordi. "It was a very simple method, but it worked. The money they were making was in the millions. How much I don't know, but it was a lot. I had to do some of the logistics for them at the risk of my life."

"And the people who were using you were doing the transport. Who were these people?"

"I can't say."

"I think you can." Jordi lightly tapped the knife on the table.

"This is going to get me in trouble," Abdouelle said, looking helpless.

"When do you want the trouble? Now or later?"

Abdouelle looked across at the tall blond man who hadn't moved, his eyes looking more menacing than ever. He hesitated then said, "It was Shafi Khanoum."

"Where is this Shafi Khanoum?"

"Dead."

"Dead? How?"

"Shafi Khanoum was a gangster in this area. He was losing power. The rumor is that last year one of the shipments went bad. The explosives blew up a corporate jet. He continued to operate, but not at the same level. Other gangs moved in and then a couple of weeks ago one of the gangs shot him."

"You're lying."

"I'm not," Abdouelle insisted. "I was just leaving his place when they came for him, but I managed to get out before they arrived. I was lucky because they may have also shot me, but I'm even more lucky because I don't have him around any more demanding that I do all those risky things."

"Did you get a look at the men who shot him?"

"No, I left before they came."

"So you can't describe them?" Jordi asked.

"No," Abdouelle answered.

"Do you believe the killing was the result of a fight between rival gangs?"

"Yes."

"You mentioned a man last week who was here. What did he do?"

"He went over to the apartment of Khanoum, but it had already been cleared out. It was empty and he did not find anything. There were people who did not like that man being there. This part of town is full of gangs and rival gangs and they don't like unknown people coming into their neighborhood. My advice is that he doesn't go sticking his nose around any more. Gangs don't like that. If people like him keep causing trouble they will hunt him down and take care of him. And I might say the same advice for you."

"Well, thank you for taking such a strong interest in our safety and thank you for your information."

Something clicked in Abdouelle's brain. He had forgotten to turn on the video camera. He moved his leg to the side of the desk where he felt the switch, lifted his knee and moved the switch upwards.

Jordi continued, "Mr. Abdouelle, this conversation never took place. If we hear about it anywhere through our network, we will find you. Do you understand?" At that Jordi lifted the knife and stuck it strongly into Abdouelle's desk. Laszlo took two steps forward and stood next to Jordi.

Abdouelle looked at both of them, sweat pouring down his face and said, "Yes, this conversation never took place."

"Thank you, Mr. Abdouelle, for your kind hospitality."

Jordi nodded to Laszlo who opened the door. They walked through the reception area. Seated behind the desk was a heavily made-up woman with bleached blond hair. Saying nothing to her, they exited the office and walked quickly down the street.

Abdouelle sat soaked in sweat, his wrinkled business suit damp under the armpits. He had revealed too much. The man asking him the questions was frightening, but the other man standing by the door was as cold as steel. He wondered if the video worked.

And if it did, whether he should destroy the tape.

CHAPTER 36

Spiros answered on the first ring. "Who is it?"

"Your fairy godmother."

"You are not following procedures." Spiros knew it was Yass. Yass and Turk had been sent down the previous night when he had lost contact with Valentine. "So what have you found?"

"A lot of interesting things," Yass said, knowing that Spiros was nervous.

"What?" Spiros demanded.

"Your man, this Collins, got himself banged up, is in the hospital, and will probably be there for some days." Through some local people in Llanca, Yass had found out that a car, probably that stupid Valentine, had hit Collins and put him in the hospital.

"In the hospital?" Spiros asked in disbelief.

"Yes, and I hear he has a girlfriend who is there night and day."

"And Valentine? Where is Valentine?" asked Spiros.

"In hell. Your chosen one is in hell."

"What do you mean?" Spiros demanded, his voice high pitched. Yass liked it when Spiros panicked. Besides, it was Spiros who had decided to send Valentine here on his own and Valentine had screwed up. He would never have trusted that erratic idiot himself. Spiros was likely to be in trouble with *Le Patron*.

Yass spoke. "I mean exactly what I mean. Valentine is in hell. Dead. He drove the rental car off a cliff, the rental car you got for him, and burned to a crisp."

The line stayed silent for quite some time while Yass waited. Finally he heard Spiros clear his throat and attempt confidence. "Why don't you and Turk get out of there? Our task was only to observe, and now Collins ends up in the hospital and we have one of our own men dead. Let's cover our tracks and leave town."

"I will think about it," said Yass slowly.

"No, Yass. Get out of there now."

A trace of fear remained in Spiros' voice so Yass continued, "Maybe, but Turk and I need a little holiday. We'll hang around here for a while."

Spiros took a deep breath. "What do you want, Yass?"

"Some cash."

"How much?"

"Ten thousand dollars." But then, having Turk indebted to him wasn't a bad idea either. "No, make it twenty—ten for me and ten for Turk.

"OK. Just get back here."

"We are on our way, but you'd better have the money ready." Yass turned off his mobile phone and signaled Turk to start the car. "We are heading back to Nice. But let's stop at the hospital first. Visiting hours are still on."

* * *

One hundred fourty-four ceiling tiles. Ten stitches per inch on the white sheet hem. Eight dents in the metal railing of his bed.

It was Thursday, and Justin was going to implode if he had to stay in the hospital a minute longer. The previous day he had been up and around, much to the nurse's displeasure. The drip had been removed from his arm, and while he still had a headache, it was not as bad as Wednesday.

As he swung his legs over the side of the bed and attempted to stand up, a man walked through the door. He wore jeans, brown hiking shoes, a blue shirt and a black leather jacket. He had Mediterranean features, and Justin noticed a pronounced scar down the left side of his face.

"Can I help you?" Justin asked.

The man stood there for a few moments staring at Justin, expressionless. Justin wondered vaguely if the scar moved when the man smiled. If the man smiled. "Are you Collins?"

"Yes, why do you ask?"

The man didn't answer.

"Who are you?" Justin asked.

"A doctor."

The man stared at Collins for a few more seconds and then turned and walked out into the hall. Justin sat back on the bed, his head spinning. The man didn't look like the other doctors, even off-duty. And how did he know his name?

Justin tried to stand up again, and this time he felt less wobbly on his feet. Another man walked through the door.

It was Jordi.

"*Hombre*, are you going for a walk?"

Justin laughed and said, "Yes, I'm going to walk the twenty kilometers back to Llanca."

"You might try hitchhiking instead," Jordi replied. "How are you feeling?"

"Better. All day Wednesday I thought my head was going to split apart, but now it's just a small headache. Seriously, I would like to go back to Llanca."

"What do the doctors say?"

"They say I need rest and that I should not move for a few days. They want to keep me here to make sure it happens. I have a sneaking suspicion they just want to run up my hospital bill."

"You could consider this hospital time a little holiday. Why don't you stay?"

"I can rest just as well at home. They are feeding me and giving me some pills and that's about all. I can take the pills at home and I have food at home. I'm going crazy with nothing to do. At least at home I can look out at the sea." Justin looked down at his hospital gown. "And the fashion's getting to me."

Jordi thought about this and knew it was easier to keep surveillance on Justin if he were in Llanca. Whoever that 'gang' was, they could come back. He was sure that it was Laszlo Vartek who took care of that nervous English guy, but who knew if there were more to come? Yes, it did make sense to get Justin out of here.

"OK. Get dressed. We are going."

Justin went to a cupboard in the room where his clothes were hanging: a t-shirt, shorts and running shoes. The hospital had washed his t-shirt and shorts, but they were torn. He looked a mess when he put them on, but it beat leaving in the open-backed gown. They walked down the corridor to the main reception desk. Jordi addressed the nurse on duty, speaking Catalan.

"Mr. Collins would like to check out today."

"Do you think this is a hotel?" she said. "He is supposed to stay and rest for a few more days."

"He can rest at home. He wants to go."

"Just wait here a minute," she said. She scurried off down the hall and into one of the side rooms.

Within seconds a doctor emerged and greeted them at the desk. He was straightforward and to the point. "We advise that Mr. Collins should not leave."

"He wants to leave," said Jordi. "He is very appreciative of the care you have given him. Now let's settle any paperwork if necessary and please prescribe any medicine he needs."

"And who are you?" the doctor asked.

"My name is Jordi Pujols from Llanca."

At that the doctor stood quiet for a moment, shifting the position of his shoulders. "Please wait a minute, Mr. Pujols. I will write out a prescription," he said. He left and returned momentarily. "Please remember that Mr. Collins should not move around much in the next few days. He should have plenty of fluids and sleep. He is not in danger, but his head took quite a shock. These pills," he said, handing Jordi two small pieces of paper, "should help with the pain and inflammation. And these pills," he said, indicating the bottom sheet, "will help him sleep."

"Thank you, doctor," replied Jordi.

Justin understood part of the conversation. Jordi signaled to him to exit the hospital, but Justin walked over to the doctor and nurse and said in French, "*Merci beaucoup.*" He turned and followed Jordi out of the hospital. Jordi's car was parked out front—in the doctor's parking space.

"Are you feeling OK?" Jordi asked. He pulled onto the main highway to Llanca. "Yes, a little bit dizzy, but I'll make it."

"Do you remember any more of what happened, how you got here?"

"Yes, some of the details. I was jogging on a dirt road leading to one of the quarries west of Llanca. A car came speeding around the bend. He didn't slow down, so I had to jump. I went flying over the side down toward a gully. I must have hit my head on a rock. After that everything goes a bit fuzzy until waking up on Wednesday. How I got from the hills to the hospital, I don't know. I have a vague recollection of a man, but I'm not sure."

"Well, in any case you are OK." Jordi checked his rearview mirror and took a hand off the wheel, hanging the other arm out his window. "By the way, I heard the good news about Gloria and yourself. Congratulations."

"Thank you. I'm very happy, all this accident stuff aside. By the way, could I ask you something?"

"Sure."

"Back there at the hospital you were talking to the doctor. I don't think he knew you, but he changed his mind about me leaving when you mentioned your name."

"Is that a question? Maybe he got me mixed up with someone else. No, you just need to learn Catalan."

Justin knew he needed to improve his Catalan but doubted the rest. He knew that Jordi had a reputation. These towns and villages along the Costa Brava were small places where everyone knew everyone. He was well aware that there was respect for Jordi in Llanca, but in Figueras too?

"Has anything been going on in Llanca?" Justin asked.

"No, not really. Just a typical July, full of tourists."

Conversation ended after this, and Justin was a bit relieved when they finally reached his small house on the cliff. Jordi stopped the car while Justin got out.

"Jordi, thank you for bringing me back here."

Jordi waved in acknowledgment and drove away. Justin went inside and saw that a telephone had been installed. The telephone company existed after all. He pulled up a chair by the phone, dialed the bank in Llanca, and asked for Gloria. She came to the phone. "Hello, beautiful woman," he said. "This is just to let you know that I'm home in Llanca."

"What?" she replied. "You were supposed to stay in the hospital for a few more days."

"I got bored. And I wanted to be closer to you."

"Oh, Justin, you are so hard-headed."

"Can you come by after work?"

"Of course. I will bring some dinner."

"Thanks Gloria. I love you."

"I love you, too."

Without returning the phone to its cradle, he dialed a number in Geneva.

"Stefan Von Portzer."

"Hello Stefan, this is Justin."

"How are you doing?"

"I had an accident. Had to dodge a speeding car and ended up hitting my head against a rock. A small concussion with a few days in the hospital, but I'm home now and feeling better."

"I am sorry to hear that but glad that you are doing better."

Stefan's voice sounded rather matter-of-fact, but Justin went on. "I just called to find out if you have found out anything about the company in Bucharest, or if Doby has come up with anything."

"We have been investigating, but it will take time. I know that the papers you found in Amsterdam appeared abnormal, but perhaps it was just some crazy coincidence. My own hypothesis is that some underworld gang was transporting things and using that airplane to do it. I will continue to look into it, but don't worry too much on your end. It's finished. You need to rest, heal, and spend time with that beautiful young woman you told me about."

"Stefan, I didn't tell you, but we are getting married. September seventh. Can you come?"

"Well, congratulations. Yes, I will be there. Perhaps I can come a day early so we might have a chance to talk—in case I do find out any more information."

"I'd like that, Stefan."

"Don't worry. Leave everything to me."

"Thanks. I appreciate it."

"Take care of yourself, Justin."

"You too. Bye."

"Good bye."

Justin rested back in his chair. A few minutes later there was a knock on the door. To Justin's surprise, Sanchez, one of Jordi's friends, was standing there with two boxes full of groceries. He nodded at Justin, set them in the kitchen, handed Justin a few current English newspapers and magazines, and left.

Justin was getting tired of all this silence. He picked up one of the newspapers and a glass of water and walked out to his small back patio overlooking the sea. He chose a comfortable chair in the shade. His head still hurt, and he started to wonder if he had done the right thing leaving the hospital so early.

For some time he sat on the chair looking out at the crystal blue sea, letting the sun warm his bruised skin. No, this *was* much better than the hospital room.

Finally he picked up a newspaper and turned to the business section. As he checked out several share prices, one short article across the page caught his attention.

The board of directors of the EuroVinco Corporation, the European electronics manufacturing and distribution company, announced through a press release that the current Chief Executive Officer, Mr. Jean Roseau, decided to resign from this position. Mr. Roseau, 63, has headed EuroVinco for the past three years. Outside analysts attribute this move to the fact that the results of EuroVinco Holding have slipped over the previous four quarters. EuroVinco, which has been one of the most successful European companies in the electronics industry, has run into cash flow and expense problems. The board of directors did not announce a replacement for Mr. Roseau. Rumors circulate about a potential partnership with Unipac, the well-known U.S. manufacturer of electronics equipment. Mr. Roseau has not been available for comment."

Well, things seem to be heating up, Justin thought, turning to the sports page.

CHAPTER 37

Yass and Turk made it back to Nice and headed straight for the building where Spiros was working. When they walked into the office, Spiros looked surprised to see them. And worried. He looked at them both a long second and said, "*Le Patron* has called a meeting to talk about Spain. Can I ask you guys to back me up?"

"We made a business deal," Yass said. "Where is the money?"

"Look, this is serious. I don't want to lose my job. I will give you five thousand dollars if you back me up."

Yass noticed Spiros's hands were shaking. This meant he had room to negotiate. "Give us five thousand dollars each, in addition to the ten thousand each you already owe us, and then we will back you up before *Le Patron*."

"OK. I will give it to you tomorrow."

"Tomorrow is not good enough," Yass replied. "We followed your instructions and came back here right away. Pay up now. A deal is a deal."

Spiros placed his hands on his desk to keep them still—as much from anger as fear. He took a key out of his pocket and went to a filing cabinet, unlocked it, reached inside and counted out two stacks of one-hundred-dollar bills. "There, fifteen thousand each." He set the stacks in front of him, a finger on each. He stabbed at the bills in time with his words. "Now, I need your loyalty—" He picked up a pile and held it toward Yass, continuing, "—in case *Le Patron* has questions about what happened in Spain. Valentine was a loose cannon, and you need to explain that to *Le Patron* if he asks."

"Sure, sure," Yass replied. "Don't worry about it. I will back you before *Le Patron*." Yass grabbed his money from Spiros. Turk reached for his stack with a vapid grin on his face, and they left the room.

They passed an office where two hackers sat typing at computers. In another office they saw a man sitting. Yass recognized him. Ziginiglou. It looked like they had transferred him down from Paris. He and Turk went over to a coffee machine and poured themselves cups of coffee.

Spiros's telephone rang down the hall, followed by a mumbled conversation that did not make it through the office walls. As the coffee cooled down and he started to sip it, Yass saw Spiros coming out from his office, his face white.

"*Le Patron* wants to see us," Spiros said. "You two, me and

Ziginiglou." He ran his hand through his hair, almost as if to make sure his head was still there.

"He wants to see us *now*."

★ ★ ★

In the four years Doby had worked with Von Portzer, he had never been told to bring anyone to the farmhouse. Once or twice the big blond guy had been out here, the one with eyes of cold steel. He was quiet, but Doby would never want to cross his path going in the wrong direction.

Von Portzer owned the place, but Doby ran his business from it under the condition that he would do the occasional project for Von Portzer, who often stopped by to enjoy the view and drink wine on the quiet terrace.

No one besides Von Portzer and Laszlo had ever seen the equipment. Collins had seen the stuff in the barn but none of the real gear downstairs.

Doby pulled the photocopies Collins had left him from a pile of papers. He looked at his hand-written notes and began to chart out a course of research. Any research plan was just a high level roadmap, and this would change as he wound his way through different databases. It was like trying to search for obscure information on the Internet, starting at one website and ending up somewhere else. That was the nature of his search.

But he did not have much to go on here, other than several names of companies, addresses and a few telephone numbers. The company on the logo of the document was EuroVinco Trading, and he saw the names of Marché Transport, and Locomotiva Bucharesti in Romania.

He thought a moment, decided on the research methodology he would use, and then typed a command into one of the terminals on the desk. It was a high-speed workstation, ideal for moving around networks and for keeping numerous sessions open as he jumped from application to application. He started with a 'network association' methodology. It was simple: identify the relationships. Who knows who? Which relationships are the strongest? And of course, he kept his trail virtually—and actually—untraceable.

He accessed the Dutch Telecom Company and soon made it into the billing data. This included a record of each customer's calls.

He found a search screen and typed in the name of EuroVinco

Trading. He was surprised to see two companies with that name come up on the screen. He chose the one matching the telephone number on the photocopy and waited. A list of hundreds of telephone calls came up. He quickly did a data dump, transferring the information into a database in one of his workstations. He left Dutch Telecom but stayed online.

Each telephone number in his database had a country code in front of it: 44 for the U.K., 49 for Germany, 34 for Spain, 33 for France. He did a quick count with the computer and totaled all the calls that had been made over a one-year period. He then did a simple "sort" and found that no country represented more than twenty percent of the calls. He performed an additional sort to determine a frequency of matching telephone numbers, while arranging them in descending order. In a few seconds he had his answer.

In identifying the most frequently called numbers, three were for the Netherlands, two for France, one for Germany, one for England. Eighty percent of the calls had been made to these seven numbers. That was enough for a first analysis.

The number most frequently called was for somewhere in the South of France. He needed to look up the exact location.

He spent the next hour setting up his program and went upstairs to get a cup of coffee while his system did its work. The program was written to access different directory assistance databases around the world, calling into and matching databases with names and addresses, again taking the data and storing it in the database in his workstation one by one as matches were found.

His 'network association' methodology was nothing more than establishing a network of telephone numbers and addresses. Who called whom? You would start with one node and find out whom someone was talking with and then go on to the next node and the next until you built up a map of relationships. In Collins's case the first node was the EuroVinco Trading Specialized Trading Department. Who had been on the other line?

After that question was answered, those most frequently called numbers became the next nodes, and then he had to find out if those next nodes were talking directly with each other. It was a case of matching numbers in databases to form a map.

It could take days to build up the map of relationships because of data base anomalies along the way.

Doby hoped this one would finish faster.

CHAPTER 38

Spiros drove. The other three watched the passing vineyards as they headed a half-hour out of Nice, eventually turning off onto a gravel road. They wound through small, sage-covered hills until they came to a *Mas*, an old stone farmhouse. They parked next to a white van that glared in the bright sun.

Two men stood next to the van smoking cigarettes. Yass recognized them as bodyguards who worked for *Le Patron:* Serge and Pierre, two infidels. *Le Patron* used them to intimidate people, but they didn't intimidate Yass. When the four got out of their car, Serge and Pierre stood at attention and signaled to them to enter the *Mas*.

They made their way inside the one-room, stone-walled building. Wooden shutters blocked light from entering the glassless windows. Everyone blinked and waited for their eyes to adjust. There were several chairs scattered around the room. The two men continued to wait outside.

Yass didn't like waiting inside, so he stepped back out. Serge, bristling with authority, told him, "You are not supposed to be out here. Go inside."

Yass looked straight at him and walked past the vehicles to sit on a stone under an old oak tree. From the shade there, he stared back at Serge and Pierre. They said nothing and continued to smoke their cigarettes. Spiros, Ziginiglou and Turk remained inside.

In a few minutes a black Citroën came speeding up the gravel road, dust billowing behind it. As the car stopped and a man opened the door, Serge and Pierre quickly crushed out their cigarettes.

Le Patron. Yass was always surprised to see how perfectly the man dressed. And he wore an air of assurance at least as well as his tailored clothes. It must be that Hollywood smile. *Le Patron* flashed that smile at them and then looked at Yass.

"We told him to wait inside, but he wouldn't," Serge said, almost pouting.

Le Patron looked at Serge and Pierre, then at Yass. He said nothing but walked across to the *Mas* and went in the front door. Serge and Pierre followed on his heels, and Yass waited a second to let them pass, then felt the gun tucked into the holster on his side and the switchblade knife in his pocket. Only then did he enter. *Le Patron* had just started to speak.

"Gentlemen. I'm glad you could all make it here. Thank you for coming."

Yass waited, his back to the door, keeping a close eye on Serge and Pierre. Everyone was standing and *Le Patron* said, "Why don't you make yourselves comfortable? Mr. Spiros, Mr. Ziginiglou, please be seated."

All the rest were left standing. Somehow Yass thought that was a good sign. Both Spiros and Ziginiglou looked nervous, and Yass could see a sheen of sweat spreading across Spiros's forehead. After a moment of uneasy silence, Spiros asked, "Why is this meeting called?"

"Oh, it's just a team meeting," *Le Patron* said. "We need to evaluate where we are and to see if we need to take any corrective actions."

"Corrective actions for what?" demanded Spiros.

"I want to go through the events of last week so that everyone understands what we could have done better and how things will be done from now on." *Le Patron* looked at Spiros and then at the others.

Le Patron stayed quiet for a moment and then said, "Let's start with Amsterdam. The auditor started something, and I suppose it was unavoidable. It was a tactical error to put the Specialized Trading Department in the same building as EuroVinco Trading. But Mr. Ziginiglou, I thank you for your assistance and that of our three consultants who removed the auditor. The office was quickly vacated and that was well done. As far as I understand no one has even found the auditor's remains."

Yass liked being called a 'consultant' and being commended by *Le Patron*. But at the mention of the auditor, his throat had gone a bit dry. The last time he saw the fat man floating in the canal, he thought he had noticed a faint movement under the surface of the water. But they had kept an eye on the canal to make sure nothing surfaced.

Le Patron continued, "Then there was the project in London. I'm pleased to have received the report. The negative thing was the security guard, but up to this point the investigations of Scotland Yard have led to nothing. It's quite a bureaucratic organization, and the case will probably be lost in paperwork. I understand this incident was unavoidable and feel that it was handled as well as was possible."

"Then there was the incident of this Mr. Collins." As he mentioned this name, *Le Patron's* breezy narrative voice solidified into distinct disapproval. He leaned back on his polished heels and put his hands into the pinstriped pockets of his pants. "First he goes to Paris. How he found out about Marché Transport it is hard to know. Mr. Ziginiglou, was anything left in the office that would have directed him to Paris?"

"No sir. The office was cleaned out as instructed," Ziginiglou answered, knowing that Marché Transport did not get everything out on that weekend and had to go back for a second trip. He hoped *Le Patron* did not know this.

Le Patron continued, "Well, in any case, Collins went to Paris, but it did not lead him anywhere, and he eventually went back to Spain where he has been living. Thanks to our two consultants here for finding out this information for us." He turned and nodded his head at Yass and Turk.

Yass noticed that Turk had that ridiculous smile on his face. Luckily the mustache hid most of it.

"The unfortunate thing about all of this is the potential visibility it is creating. I now expect extreme caution and vigilance. I have business affairs that are in progress and they cannot be jeopardized. I also want all my instructions followed. Do you all understand this?"

Both Spiros and Ziginiglou nodded their heads up and down saying, "Yes, sir," and Spiros added, "We understand."

"I can see that you all understand. Now, there is one last problem we should talk about. We are missing Mr. Valentine, and I understand he ran into some problems in Spain. Mr. Spiros, can you explain this?"

"He went to Spain and didn't follow orders," Spiros answered.

"What were the orders?"

"To stay low and stay invisible, just to keep surveillance on Collins. Nothing more."

"And what happened?"

"We don't know," Spiros said.

"The way I understand it, Mr. Spiros, is like this: Valentine went after Collins and tried to hit him with a car and somehow Valentine got himself killed. Now, I ask you the question, Mr. Spiros. Is that following my instructions?"

"Well no, but I told you that he didn't follow instructions."

"Think about it. Valentine was a poor choice to send to Spain. He is the one person who could have endangered things. Isn't that so, Mr. Spiros?"

"Yes, but I thought we might need Yass and Turk here for some work, so I sent Valentine down there." Spiros turned to Yass and said, "Isn't that right, Yass? You know it wasn't an easy decision. I did my best. Don't you agree?"

Le Patron turned and asked, "Yass, what do you think?"

"Valentine was crazy. He could be used for some jobs but never on his own. You would have to be nuts to send him on a job like that."

"Yass, what are you doing?" Spiros cried out. "The money. I will lose my job!"

Le Patron said, "I think we have heard enough. This is a problem we don't need."

He turned to the others, making prolonged eye contact with each of them, and said, "Not one slip-up from here on." *Le Patron* pulled a gun from under his coat, aimed it at Spiros and pulled the trigger. There was a loud thump as Spiros fell backwards off the chair. His head bounced hard against the stone floor where it remained motionless.

No one moved. Ziginiglou started to shake quietly. He had been sitting next to Spiros, and his shirt was spotted with blood. He wiped some of it from the side of his face.

Le Patron said, "Now, I think we understand the point. I cannot, in any case, have more screw-ups. Everything shall be done quietly and discretely. Spiros used poor judgment. It could have greatly jeopardized my plans. None of you can afford to do that any more."

He looked around once again. Yass stood still, quiet as a stone and almost relaxed. *Le Patron* handed a key to Serge. "You two take care of that."

Serge and Pierre immediately moved and lifted the body and carried it outside behind the *Mas*. In the yard was an old stone well with a metal cover and a lock. Serge unlocked it and opened the cover. They lifted the body and dropped it into the black hole; a few seconds later there was a thud. After closing and relocking the metal cover they went inside the *Mas* and handed the key to *Le Patron*.

He put the key in his pocket and spoke. "Mr. Ziginiglou, I want you to take over Spiros's job. Move your accountants from Amsterdam to the Nice office, and they can resume work from there. The two computer engineers will report to you. Are you ready to take on this new role?"

"Yes sir," Ziginiglou said, struggling to enunciate both words.

"Thank you, Mr. Ziginiglou. Now, we have potentially started something with Collins, but perhaps not. I don't want him to interfere. If he stays in Spain, fine, just leave him alone. Ziginiglou, we have used an independent agency in Barcelona to help us from time to time. Ask them to keep a full-time watch on Collins. Yass and Turk, I want you to check in consistently with that agency."

Le Patron straightened his starched collar and finished, "If he starts to cause any problems, then, and only then, will we deal with him."

CHAPTER 39

Llanca, Spain
August 14th

He was standing in front of the whale tank again. Its thick glass wall dulled the words of the people banging on it. When Justin reached out his hands and pressed an ear to the glass to listen, he noticed something. They were no longer drowning.

There was no water inside.

He awoke trembling and held his temples, glad at least that the concussion headaches had ceased.

Though the pain in his head at the moment was worse. It was a pain no pill could ease, though he had thought it finally distant—a star always there in his sky.

Two stars.

Whether the sun shone or not, they were there beyond the blue.

★ ★ ★

August flew by. Gloria had more or less single handedly seen to the wedding preparations. After being shooed from the Butler parlor where acres of pale fabric lay draped across the furniture, a bemused Justin had been told by James, "For a Spanish woman a wedding is like a kitchen. The men stay out."

Justin and Gloria had spent weekends in Barcelona, and on those visits, Justin stayed at the Butlers' house enjoying his discussions with James. While the two of them talked business, Gloria and her mother visited shops, sent out invitations, and ticked steadily away at the wedding to-do list.

When in Llanca, Justin went faithfully once a week to the single cyber café and looked for any e-mail messages from Doby. His in-box was always empty, and he had begun to wonder if Doby was doing anything

On the morning of September 6th, the day before the wedding, Justin went to the cyber café and logged on to his site, and was surprised to see a message from Doby. It read:

From: Doby
To: Justin

Justin, still performing market research. Have found some linkages, but nothing conclusive. This will take some time and am not sure where it will lead. Am motivated. Will let you know when I have found more info.
Regards,
Doby

Justin typed a reply.

From: Justin
To: Doby

Dear Doby,
Thanks for your message and for what you are doing. You told me it would take time, and I understand. Please don't feel you have to spend too much energy on this. I am unsure how far I want to push the evidence we discussed. My life is moving in a new direction and I am looking forward to marrying a wonderful woman tomorrow.
Best,
Justin

When Justin sent the message it immediately appeared in Doby's inbox. Since he was sitting in front of his computer at that moment, Doby read it.

He actually had more information than he had told Justin but did not want to create any false expectations. Perhaps Justin was right and this would not, or should not, lead anywhere. Doby had built up his relationship map, and everything seemed to point to an office in Nice, France. Now that he had pinpointed that node, the next methodology he planned to use was one he called 'gold mining.' This was more complex and difficult than the first. He had to find out which Internet service provider the Nice office was using, what firewall software was loaded on the computer and several other bits of information.

It would be a delicate and time-consuming operation. But as he had e-mailed Justin, he was motivated.

★ ★ ★

Later that afternoon, Stefan Von Portzer arrived in Llanca, ready to attend the wedding scheduled for the following day.

Justin took Stefan to a small restaurant in a village about five kilometers from Llanca on the road to Figueras, one that specialized in roast lamb served with Spanish red wine. It was an unpretentious place with so many green vines hanging from the ceiling that diners felt they were eating in a garden.

Von Porzter watched a lamb roasting in a brick fireplace that occupied the middle of the restaurant. He looked back at Justin, the one-liter carafe of red wine between them, and asked, "How are you feeling?"

Justin reached for the bottles of oil and vinegar and sprinkled them on his salad.

"I'm not sure," Justin answered truthfully. "I tossed and turned all night, or what little I had of it. There is a guy in the village named Jordi. He and some of his friends took me out last night for a sort of bachelor's party."

"So you got, what do they say in Britain, lacquered?" Stefan smiled.

"That was the idea, but I ended up being the designated driver, bringing them home somewhere around four o'clock in the morning. We did have fun. They're a wild group—even the village barber."

"I suppose I should be more specific: how do you feel about the wedding?"

"Some months ago I wondered if I could face marriage again after all that has happened." Justin watched the lamb turning on its spit, amazed that part of that flesh was on his plate and it did not bother him. "But then I look at Gloria and wonder how could I not?"

"Well Justin, to each his own. My philosophy in life was to sample the desserts, but no woman was ever able to bring me to the dinner table."

Justin laughed. "Stefan, I'm sure there are many women that would like to bring you to the table. I've wondered if you could live on a constant diet of Viennese strudel."

"You are probably right," Von Portzer acknowledged with a slight lift of his wine glass, "but I am too old to consider marriage. I once did when I was in my early twenties." He stared at the stem of his glass, but Justin could tell that was not what he was seeing. "The one and only woman I really loved married a rich banker. Since then I have never recovered." He made light of this with a slight flourish.

"Are you sure it wasn't just an excuse?" Justin asked.

"Well maybe. But I have been happy. Lonely sometimes, but some people can be even more lonely in marriage.”

Justin paused for a moment then said, “Stefan, thank you for coming. It means a lot to me that you are here.”

“I am glad to be here. I have heard that your young woman with the green eyes is very attractive.”

“How do you know she had green eyes?” Justin tried to recall if he had mentioned them.

Stefan realized that Laszlo Vartek had described Gloria to him, so he said, “You told me when we met at the airport in Zurich.” He leaned toward his meal, shifting the subject a bit. “Remember, a bride is always the most beautiful woman in the world on her wedding day, although after that she may become fat and ugly.”

“You are so encouraging.”

“Don’t tell me that I didn’t warn you.”

★ ★ ★

When the coffee came, Stefan said, “There is one thing I wanted to tell you not related to the marriage.”

Justin’s face tensed and he asked, “What did your man find out?”

“We looked in a couple of directions. First I had someone visit Bucharest on your behalf. He managed to destroy a building, which is a long story and incidental. He discovered that the shipment came from a munitions factory. It appears they were dealing with questionable clients—a gang—who were trafficking weapons and explosives. These items were brought to a distribution point in Paris. They used business jets to transport their goods, mainly to the Middle East and North Africa.”

“Are you telling me that there were explosives on that airplane?”

“Yes. It appears to have been a convenient way to transport them. The shipment should have been flown to Malta and then ferried over to Tunisia or Algeria. We are not sure. A business jet flying a well-known American industrialist would have likely avoided an intense customs inspection in Paris or Malta, so it would have been a relatively risk free contraband.”

“How do you know?”

“Besides our investigation in Bucharest where we found evidence of what was in the shipment, Doby found information on a small group of people who ran a department in EuroVinco Amsterdam. We think they provided materials for terrorist groups in the Middle East.”

"The Specialized Trading Department?" Justin asked, surprised.

"It appears that a person working for EuroVinco in Nice was running this department somewhere in the EuroVinco accounting structure, a Mr. Schneider. You gave me his name, but he just disappeared. He probably suspected that things were getting hot, so he discontinued his operation and fled the scene. Doby found evidence that this department in Amsterdam served to arrange shipments of anything anybody wanted and could pay for. They used Marché Transport to handle the physical logistics."

"How did Doby discover all this?"

"As I told you before, Doby is an exceptional investigator. He is one of the best I have ever hired. He is able to get information from inside companies that is usually rather…unattainable."

Justin remained quiet, watching a tendril of ivy shift in the air as a couple opened the door and left. In a way he was relieved to finally know the reason why his wife and daughter had been killed.

In another way, he was angry. He had lost his family. Vine Industries had folded. All because some evil people had tried to smuggle explosives on a convenient plane. But why was it that they had taken the trouble to ship the explosives all the way from Romania to Paris to North Africa, rather than to North Africa directly? Aloud he asked Stefan, "Why did they ship it through Paris?"

"I really don't know. Let's suppose this company in Romania had monthly shipments to France. Many do. There is a lot of trade between Romania and France. French is the second language of many Romanians. The two governments have good relations with each other. Perhaps this company took advantage of the flow of goods between the two countries. That and terrorist groups have operations and sympathizers in Paris. Doby determined some links, although he was not able to find out what group was involved."

"I want to do something. But where do managerial skills come in when you're dealing with underground trafficking?" Justin laughed at himself bitterly.

"Justin," Stefan leaned forward, "I understand your desire for justice. If I were in your shoes I would want revenge, but it's not so easy. If you want my advice, get on with your life with Gloria. We don't live in a perfect world, and there will always be crazy groups running around all trying to do stupid things to advance their various causes."

"But, we can't do nothing. These people are murderers. I want to know who they are," Justin said, clenching his jaw.

Von Portzer quietly replied, "Honestly, it would be difficult to find out who this group was. These people break apart and configure in new ways. Look how quickly Marché Transport and this Mr. Schneider managed to vanish. Look how hard it is for our governments to track down terrorist groups. It's an impossible task. You could spend a lifetime investigating and eventually only find out that they were the radical wing of a splinter group of a radical splinter group or something like that.

Justin had to admit the logic of this. Stefan knew that and went on, "If you went after them for vengeance, you would probably never find them. As I said, most likely they don't exist in the same form as a year ago. They will have disbanded, fragmented and realigned with other groups or started new ones. These kinds of people are international thugs, nothing more. They change alliances all the time. You definitely do not have the means to find them, and it's not in your character to take revenge using the same means they use—violence and terror."

Stefan reached for a cigar. "I say, get on with your life. Consider this a very tragic and unfortunate event in your past. Tomorrow you will have an amazing woman walking down the aisle of a church to be your wife. Be there. Devote your life to her. Love her."

CHAPTER 40

Justin arrived early at the chapel of the Castle de Perelada. When he walked inside, he took a deep breath—both for air and for the fragrance of the lovely flowers. At the ends of each wooden pew was fastened a cluster of jasmine and white lilies. Gloria had kept things simple but had used enough flowers to make the stone walls appear soft. He fingered his own boutonnière of matching petals and retreated to a corner to watch the guests arrive.

Most were Gloria's family and friends, and Justin knew them well enough to feel they were his as well. Several of Justin's friends were there besides Stefan Von Portzer. Charles Graves and his wife had flown down from London, and Justin's stockbroker from Geneva even showed up along with his wife, glad to take advantage of a long weekend to drive around the Costa Brava. Jordi, Pascual, Sanchez and Eusebi were there, looking uncomfortable at having to be in a church.

Pascual took a seat next to Jordi and said, "I hope the priest won't be too long. I prefer burials to weddings. At least the message is short."

Jordi smiled. "Yes, my friend, but wait for the food and drinks, and take a look at all the beautiful women. That's why I prefer weddings."

Señora Pascual came up and sat behind both of them, arms folded and eyes on the backs of their heads. Both her son and Jordi sat up straighter and discontinued their discussion.

On the first row of the old wooden pews, Señora Butler sat by her children, twisting a lacey handkerchief between her fingers.

The scent of flowers mingled with the smell of strong Spanish soap and cologne as the chapel warmed up. The organist took her place and everyone shuffled to silence as the chapel filled with the wedding march and Gloria entered, hand resting on her father's arm.

Everyone stood up in silence and smiles as Gloria walked towards the altar where Justin was waiting. Her long red hair hung to the middle of her back underneath a white veil, and her dress—simple but elegant—showed her curves to fine advantage. James left her with Justin, giving him a long look, both stern and gentle.

The Presbyterian minister from Barcelona performed the ceremony in English and Catalan, highlighting the beauty of marriage as the candles burned lower.

★ ★ ★

Afterwards, in the castle garden, guests lingered over drinks and a long wedding feast, emptying the laden tables down to garnishes. Live music, laughter, and alcohol moved the evening toward dusk.

At one point late in the dinner, Stefan Von Portzer was discussing Spanish history with the newlyweds.

Von Portzer, well schooled in the country's general history, asked a more specific question. "And Llanca, do you happen to know what the name of this village means?"

Señora Pascual walked up to them at this moment and promptly answered—correctly assuming she was the only one present who knew—"Llanca means like lance, but is spear—Catalan for spear." She made a jabbing motion with her arms, as if aiming for a shark in water. "We have—how you say, legs?"

Everyone exchanged confused and amused glances.

Justin smiled. "If only for my morning runs, I do hope so." Gloria laughed.

"Ah, you joker," Señora Pascual shook her finger at him, thinking a second. "Ah, no legs, *arms*. Jacket of arms, yes."

"Ah, civic heraldry," Stefan nodded, carefully not correcting her use of 'jacket' instead of 'coat.' "I always find such things fascinating. And how are these spears depicted?"

Señora Pascual, approving of his genial interest, answered, "You see square like this," she made a topless square by forming 'L's with her thumbs and forefingers, "then turn to make so." She turned the "square" a bit to the left, until it more or less resembled a…

"Diamond?" Gloria asked, holding up her hand and its ring.

Señora Pascual nodded, continuing, "Water in bottom of diamond. The sea." She lifted her head to look at the Mediterranean, gone indigo in the crepuscule light. "And from it rise three *llances*, these spears. One in middle, tallest. All point to a crown that hang above. This," she finished, addressing her rapt audience, "is what for Llanca is named."

★ ★ ★

"Why three spears, do you think?" Gloria asked him later, lips at his ear as they danced to the sounds of guitar and Jordi entertaining the unmarried ladies.

"And why pointing at the crown?" he asked back. "I don't know, but trust Señora Pascual to have local history at her fingertips." He ran his hand down her back to where it began to curve. "I prefer having you at my fingertips."

She lifted her head from his shoulder and held his eyes with her own in such an answer that all questions left his head.

The couple left the castle grounds hand-in-hand and got into a rented racing-green Jaguar that Justin drove north toward France.

★ ★ ★

"Who is it?" Ziginiglou asked of the phone receiver.

"You tried to call me an hour ago. What did you want?" demanded a cold voice.

Ziginiglou knew it was *Le Patron*. He had tried to call and update him on Yass and Turk's latest trip to Spain. Ever since that eventful meeting in the *Mas*, Ziginiglou had done everything possible to ensure that what *Le Patron* wanted, *Le Patron* got.

The new job was full of revelations. Ziginiglou had found out much more about *Le Patron's* operations, including one in California. Still, he knew that certain information was kept from him.

Ziginiglou also continued to manage the accounting group. Since relocating from Amsterdam to Nice, they had taken on more responsibilities and now managed *Le Patron*'s different bank accounts.

Ziginiglou's worries were increasing as rapidly as his responsibilities. He was determined that Spiros' fate should not be his own. He would do everything in his power to keep open communications with *Le Patron*. He would rather be an irritation than a disappointment.

"This is just to give you the latest update on California and Spain."

"So give it," *Le Patron* said.

"First, our agents in San Jose have successfully tapped the telephone line in the Santa Cruz house. They are monitoring all telephone conversations."

"Good. What about the son-in-law?"

"They are working on it."

"Good. Tell them to get it done fast. And make sure you listen carefully to all the conversations. If there is anything sensitive, any talk about EuroVinco or Unipac, you let me know."

"Yes sir." That was of interest to Ziginiglou. Until now he had had his suspicions, but now he knew that *Le Patron* was after something. Ziginiglou went on, "The second update concerns Yass and Turk. They are currently down in Spain and are trying to keep clear of Collins's village. They are leaving surveillance to the Barcelona agency. It is doing a good job of watching Collins. One of their people has been hired as a construction worker on an apartment complex not too far from Collins's house. The man acts as liaison for Yass and Turk."

"Tell me the status."

"It is very quiet. Collins spends most of his time with his girlfriend and that is about it."

"His girlfriend?"

"Yes, he spends time with a young Spanish woman almost every evening. It looks like it is getting serious."

"What do you mean?"

Ziginiglou said, "They got married today."

Le Patron broke out in laughter. "I think we don't need to worry about Collins anymore. Tell everybody to get out of there. We can use them for better things."

The line went dead.

Ziginiglou was surprised at how quick *Le Patron* had made the decision to end the surveillance. More than that he felt a cold shiver up his spine as he thought of the tone of *Le Patron's* laugh. It had nothing to do with humor. It had a tone of irony or sadism that Ziginiglou could not identify. He thought it best not to pry but it was the kind of laugh that carried lasting undertones.

CHAPTER 41

"Good morning, gorgeous woman," Justin said, his head on his hand as he leaned over Gloria's sleepy form.
She smiled. "I hope you say that when I'm eighty."
Justin held up his right hand. "Scout's honor."
"Whose?"
He laughed and kissed her. "Translation: I promise." He kissed her again. "Truly, you are beautiful in so many ways. I love all of them."
"I love you too. And I never thought of you as such a passionate man." She poked him playfully in the belly button.
He grabbed her finger and brought it to his lips. "You bring out the best in me, what can I say? Without you I'm dull and boring."
"Well this hotel *is* a renovated monastery, I suppose..."
He broke her off with a tickle under the covers.
When she stopped laughing, she sat up and said, "Mr. Collins, I'm starving." She stretched her arms. The sheet fell to her waist, baring her breasts.
Justin gently pushed her back down. "So am I."

★ ★ ★

Some time later, the noon sun bright through the windows, Gloria slipped out of bed and said, "I am hungry—for breakfast. But, first I would like to take a shower. Do not go away."
"No worries." Justin crossed his arms behind his head and watched her perfectly crafted naked body move across the room.
When he heard the shower turn on, he lifted up the telephone and ordered most everything from the breakfast and lunch menus to be brought to the room.
Lying in bed, he decided to turn on the television for a few minutes

to catch the news. He zapped through channels in French, German, Italian, Spanish and English-speaking stations from the U.K. and North America.

He found a business TV network and saw Paul Kent, the CEO of Unipac, sitting across from the anchor who said, "Today, Unipac, the California based electronics company, announced that its acquisition of EuroVinco has been cleared by the U.S. Securities and Exchange Commission and by the European Union. We have here with us Paul Kent, the company's CEO, to tell us the latest developments."

The camera showed the face of a man in his early forties with the picture of the Unipac headquarters in California in the background.

"Good morning Mr. Kent," the announcer said.

"Good morning."

"Thank you for joining us. It seems this deal has been approved in record time. Can you tell us about the terms of the merger between Unipac and EuroVinco?"

"Yes, this is a four-for-one stock swap in which shareholders of EuroVinco will receive one share of Unipac for each of their four shares of EuroVinco."

"Some analysts are saying that the shares of EuroVinco have been overpriced by Unipac. The share price of EuroVinco has dropped over the past few weeks because of weak profit results. Do you feel the four-for-one is priced too high?"

"Actually no. Two very valuable companies are coming together, and it's a rather cost effective way for Unipac to gain a significant holding in the European market."

The anchor asked, "Some analysts have questioned whether it will be possible to bring the two companies together. Unipac is well known for its particular corporate culture, and now you are trying to come together with a European company that is quite different. Isn't this going to cost a lot?"

"We don't believe so. The management teams of the two companies have been working around the clock for about a month. We know that significant synergies can be gained through leveraging the strengths of both companies into their respective marketplaces. And overall we are not worried about differences in the corporate cultures."

"This is quite a change for Unipac which has traditionally taken a conservative approach toward buying other companies."

Paul Kent replied, "As the marketplace is aware, the board of directors of Unipac are well known for making excellent business decisions in the past, and it is expected that this will have a positive impact on our results. We feel good about the plan but know there will be challenges."

"And your plan from here?"

"As I mentioned, the management teams are meeting. We are looking to gain marketing synergies, to sell existing products cross continent. Then we will look deeper to find ways to bring together production and administration."

"So you are talking about job cuts."

"No, not at all. The overall company growth prospects look excellent and we want to keep all our people who are valuable to us. Keeping people has been a strong principle within Unipac ever since it started, and it's a core value instilled by Sam Oliver during the years he was CEO. We continue with that philosophy."

"Thank you, Mr. Kent, for joining us and we wish you much success with your new company."

"Thank you," replied Paul Kent.

As they switched to a reporter on the floor of the New York Stock Exchange, Justin saw Gloria coming out of the bathroom wrapped in a white towel. He turned off the television and said, "So they went through with it."

"They went through with what?" she asked.

Justin looked at her and lost his train of thought. "Oh, nothing important. Unipac and EuroVinco have come together." He walked over to her and held her in his arms. "But this is time to think about other kinds of mergers."

The towel dropped to the floor just as someone knocked on the door. Gloria hurried into the bathroom, giggling. Justin threw on a robe and opened the door for room service.

They ate lunch in the room and talked. Justin asked her about her family, her work, Llanca. Somehow Jordi was mentioned.

"You never told me how you got to know Jordi," Gloria said.

"I met him my first day in Llanca. He was the one who recommended that I stay at Señora Pascual's. Had I not stayed there I might never have met you." He took a sip of orange juice. "Therefore, we can blame our marriage on Jordi," he said.

She laughed. "Only if it all goes wrong."

Justin said, "Jordi's a bit mysterious, don't you think? He seems to have a lot of influence around Llanca, but I don't know why. Do you know anything about him?"

She waited for a moment then said, "I have heard about him. When he was seventeen years old, something happened to his sister."

Justin asked, "What happened?"

"She was nineteen. During the summer when the tourists come, two grown men were on holiday and they got drunk. She was working in a café and was walking home late at night after it closed. The two men grabbed her, pulled her into a small street and raped her. The next day the two men were found with their throats slit. They had been cut with something very sharp. The police never found out who did it, but that day Jordi disappeared.

"For seven years he was gone. He joined the French Foreign Legion. Many people in Llanca are proud of Jordi, and he has a reputation throughout the Costa Brava, but no one ever mentions Jordi if they talk of the two men. He is known as a protector, as a man of honor. Other things have happened since he came back to the Costa Brava. People have been helped. But he is discreet about things, and he is very respected."

"That explains the day he took me out of the hospital in Llanca. The doctor came to attention when Jordi gave his name." Justin reflected, "So Jordi has this reputation as a protector and man of honor. That's quite admirable. By the way, how is his sister?"

"It took her time to recover from what those two men did to her, if one can ever fully recover. She is now married and has three children in Barcelona."

"Children." Justin paused. "How many do you want again? A dozen?"

"Hardly," Gloria laughed. "Four or five…" She swatted at the face Justin was making and considered. "OK, three. How is that?"

"Three is my favorite number," he said.

EPILOGUE

The honeymooners went for a walk in the vineyards around the monastery-hotel. It sat on a small hill overlooking the vast vineyards that stretched for twenty kilometers from the Pyrenees Mountains to Perpignan. The grapes were ripening, each vine drooping under the weight of large purple clusters.

In the late afternoon they went back to the hotel restaurant. A magnificent old room, its tall ceilings were lined with dark wooden beams, and a large fireplace rose stone on stone at its southern end. Each table was set with a white tablecloth, bone china, a bouquet of flowers from the fields, and a single lit candle. It was romantic—too romantic—and they did not linger long over their meal, having other things on their minds.

Well past check-out time the following morning, they drove to Nice and checked into their hotel. In early evening, they drove along the coast, admiring the blue sea until they came to a small isolated beach surrounded by a pine forest. Justin parked the car and they took off their shoes and walked in the sand.

The water and sky grew dark, and small lights sparkled like stars from boats in the distance. It was now the second week of September and most of the tourists were gone. They were alone.

They sat on the sand, letting their conversation drift across the future and the past. They talked freely, openly. She asked him about Paris, about living and working there, about his feelings for Chantal.

He found it strange that she asked these questions at a time like this, and he sensed that she wanted to know him deeper, that she would not be jealous of his first love.

Gloria said, "Justin, I am sure she was special. I wish I could have met her."

"She was," he said, looking at his hands that had held Chantal. "But that is past. I now have you, and you are everything to me." He placed his hands on Gloria's face, closing his eyes as if blind and seeing her through his fingers. She closed her eyes too, letting his thumbs trace her brow bone and eyelids. When he finished, he took her hand and faced the sea again. "Fate has been good to me after all. Perhaps you are right and we do have destinies. One of mine was seeing you on that Barcelona train, asleep and angelic."

"When I saw you pay for the old man's train ticket I knew you were a kind man. And I didn't even mind you staring at me." She pinched near his ribs and he yelped sideways. She put her arms around the "injured" spot and drew him close.

He said softly, "'The good and honorable thing,' this is. She was right."

"Hmm?"

"Just a pearl of Pascual wisdom, love."

"Hmm."

A full moon climbed into the sky, shedding its deep orange skin for one of bright white and sending a beam of its light at them across the dark water.

They found a secluded little cove where they pulled off each other's clothing and swam out into the soft water, stopping to kiss and sinking to their necks. The sea lay still as a lake, all life and motion and secrets below its surface.

★ ★ ★

"Sam, it's for you," called Margaret, singing out the last vowel into a second syllable. She held the telephone out for him to come take it.

"Can you tell them I'll phone back?" he yelled, one foot in the shower and one on the tiled bathroom floor.

"It's Paul," she shouted. She heard the water go on and turned back to the receiver.

"Paul, I'll have him get back to you. He's in the shower."

"Did you say it was Paul?" she heard Sam holler from the bathroom.

"Paul, hang on a sec." She heard the water go off.

"If it's Paul, tell him I'm stopping by the office around eleven," Sam continued. "Ask him if he's free to grab a bite." The water went on again.

Two hours later, Sam walked into Paul's office. "I know I'm a few minutes early, but Margaret said you had a noon lunch meeting so I thought I'd take a chance. I'm returning your call in person," he smiled.

"No, it's fine, come in. Sit down. I wanted to talk to you about something."

Sam pulled one of the rolling gray chairs closer to Paul's executive desk and sat down.

"Can I get you a cup of coffee?" Paul asked.

"Nah, I'm fine." Sam crossed his legs and leaned back. "What did you want to talk to me about?"

"Well, it's probably good you came by. I was just looking over my schedule for the coming months and it doesn't look good." He glanced at his enormous flat desk calendar and looked up again. "I don't know how I would be able to squeeze in four weeks in Europe. I could maybe do a week, possibly two, but even that would be pushing it. There's no way I can do four."

"I know things are hectic, Paul, but without visiting at least the European headquarters of EuroVinco, we would be putting ourselves in a pretty precarious situation. The merger can't succeed if it occurs only on paper. Unipac needs to be tangible, accessible, present, at least at the beginning. If we don't send someone over, especially now, we will miss our opportunity to start this thing off on the right foot."

"I recognize that, Sam. And I couldn't agree more. It's just not feasible for me to be that presence," he persisted, shaking his head.

Sam uncrossed his legs and leaned forward. "We need to think this through, Paul. As CEO, your being in Europe would endorse EuroVinco's new position. We also need to start building ties. They need to know that Unipac has a face. After all, the people are the corporation. The ideal would be to visit every EuroVinco operation in Europe. If we don't, those offices may sense a lack of support, a lack of concern.

"I have been thinking this through, Sam, and this is what I can do. At most, I could arrange to visit head offices in London and Frankfurt, and perhaps the Nice office as well. It would be good to meet the senior managers and even get them together to set a course of action for the future. I think it would also be wise to meet with a representative of the holding companies that previously held a large share of stocks in EuroVinco and now hold stocks in Unipac."

"That's good. But don't forget to schedule in time to meet with employees also. We need them to know they are key players in the company. That they're valuable. They may have questions or legitimate concerns, and we can't dismiss those. We need to be there to hear them out, provide answers, and assuage fears."

"I couldn't have said it better. And that's why you're coming with me, at least that's what I'm requesting." Paul reached for an envelope imprinted with a travel agency's logo and handed it to Sam. "And of course you can stop in the U.K. and visit your granddaughter Anne at Cambridge."

⋆ ⋆ ⋆

Justin woke to a breeze and light entering through the curtains. He turned to look at Gloria as she slept soundly next to him, her face soft with sleep on the linen-covered pillow.

He lifted a long red strand back from her cheek and tucked it behind her ear. She snuggled her chin deeper into the down but did not wake, and Justin did not disturb her further.

Watching her, he was able to see all of his past agony and present bliss at the same moment—see and feel.

How did the adage go? There is no beauty without pain? Well, then, this beautiful moment must be surpassing, considering the pain that had preceded it.

Without wanting to, he remembered Doby's e-mail and Stefan's conversation over roasted lamb. To pursue investigations—as if he even knew about such things—would be fruitless. And Stefan was right. He was not cut out for revenge.

He wanted to preserve the peace he had now and not dwell on terrorist smugglers, or whoever had been responsible for the crash. Still, when he closed his eyes, he saw a plane bursting beneath the sun, sending its metal across the mirror of the Mediterranean, piercing the water's surface with fuselage and passengers—with the family he would always hold near his heart.

The heart he had given to Gloria.

Perhaps the best way to combat the evil that had taken Chantal and Sophie was to live well and love.

AUTHOR'S NOTE

We want our lives to be without pain, yet there are times when everyone faces unexpected events that bring difficulties of some kind. That's what happened to Justin Collins, but his event was more than just a difficulty. It was tragic. In one brief moment he loses his family, his job, and his identity. How does one recover from something like this?

In Justin's case he flees Paris, heads south toward Barcelona, and ends up in a small village on the Costa Brava. There he goes through a time of healing. He even falls in love again, maybe too quickly, but his greatest desire is to get on with a new life.

This story is an example of how redemption is possible even in the worst of events. It is not to say that the pain will completely go away, for injuries create scars and we carry them to the end of our lives. But it seems we can find some level of deliverance from life's difficult moments.

With Justin, he wants a conclusion so that he can get on with his new life, but it doesn't happen. That's how it is sometimes. When we think we have put an agony behind us, it can raise its ugly head and we have to deal with it in a new way.

In *Squeeze* (Blue Fate 4), Justin finds himself in an unimaginable dilemma that will force him to make choices. The situation he finds himself in is not of his own choosing. In other words, fate is more than chance.

After you complete the book, I'd love to hear your afterthoughts. What would you do if you were Justin?

Cass Tell
Costa Brava, Spain

Your opinion is important to me!

I hope you enjoyed my book and I'd love to receive your feedback.
As the book is still fresh in your mind, please leave some comments
or a review on any of the following websites:

Amazon — www.amazon.com
Barnes & Noble — www.barnesandnoble.com
Goodreads — www.goodreads.com

And I invite you to visit my website www.casstell.com to find out
more details about all books in the Blue Fate series and my other
books.

Thank you!

www.ingramcontent.com/pod-product-compliance
Lightning Source LLC
Chambersburg PA
CBHW050341110726
47899CB00007B/2589